Other Titles by Keisha 'WriteNow' Allen

*Worth the Weight: A Love Like No Other*

Co-author of *Black Women Win: Stories to Celebrate, Honor Salute, and Acknowledge Black Women across the Globe.*

# THE *Love* ENTHUSIAST

## A Novel

KEISHA 'WRITENOW' ALLEN

THE LOVE ENTHUSIAST

This book is a work of fiction. Names, characters, and incidents either are the products of the author's imagination or are used fictitiously, and any resemblance to actual persons, living or dead, events, or locales is entirely coincidental.

THE LOVE ENTHUSIAST

Paperback ISBN: 978-1-7355789-2-7
ebook ISBN: 978-1-7355789-3-4

Published by Kreative Kreations Publishing, LLC
Lauderhill, FL

Printed in the United States of America
First edition: October 2023

Cover Design by: Daniel Flagel
Editing by: Brenna Bailey-Davies
Interior Layout by: Jose Pepito

# CONTENTS

# A LETTER FROM THE AUTHOR

Has it already been two years since I published my first story? How time flies! I know it seems like I've forgotten about you, my dear reader, but I wouldn't do that. I've missed you, but I wanted to deliver a story you could appreciate. I think Iya, aka Amina's story, is sure to deliver.

I originally intended to make *The Love Enthusiast* a short story, but I quickly realized creativity doesn't always follow instructions. I even had plans to scrap it. I wasn't sure if people would be interested in reading about an older woman's journey to self-discovery, but the story soon took on a life of its own. After taking a step back, I now appreciate this story more than ever. It has reassured me that nothing is impossible, especially if we don't give up ourselves.

In this story, you'll find some of the same characters from Worth the Weight and some new friends too. If you enjoyed *Worth the Weight: A Love Like No Other*, you'll love Anisa's mother, Amina's story. So, without further ado, I present to you, *The Love Enthusiast*! I'd love to hear your thoughts about this story, so be sure to drop me a line. You can email me at www.keishawritenowallen.com. Until then, be well.

"To those who found a way to make love work,
even when it seemed impossible."

# PROLOGUE

## Amina's Love Burden

You know what they say about an idle mind? Well, sitting in the lobby of the therapist's office gave me too much time to think, and I swear, the devil was having his way with me. I scrolled through my phone, stared out the window of the high-rise office, adjusted my dress for the hundredth time, and pushed back the cuticles of my already perfectly manicured nails.

*What the hell am I doing here*, I silently repeated.

I had gone through my insurance's directory and gotten recommendations from one of my closest friends. Although I initially wanted a woman therapist, Dr. Leon Blackwell came highly recommended and had managed to squeeze me in at the last minute. As I stood up to flee the premises, the door creaked open.

"Mrs. Thompkins?" he greeted.

I turned around to face the voice that beckoned to me, and I froze. It was too late to turn back now.

I plastered on a smile and stared at the tall, handsome stranger before me. His hair was almost completely gray, and I imagined I might add a few more grays to his head before he was done with me.

After a moment, he cleared his throat. "Umm, excuse me, Mrs. Thompkins. Are you okay?"

I nodded and adjusted my dress … again. I awkwardly added, "I think so Dr. Blackwell, but hey, that's why I'm here to see you."

We both laughed before he motioned for me to follow him.

I followed him to the small room in the back. He opened the door, and I glanced around. I immediately spotted *the chair* in the middle of the room. It was the armless chaise that I'd seen many therapists use on television. The one you laid on to bare the deepest, darkest parts of your soul. The place where you shared things that would make your daddy roll over in his grave. I quickly scanned the rest of the room and zeroed in on a desk and a standalone chair in the corner.

"Feel free to have a seat," he said and made his way over to his chair opposite the chair I was supposed to use to surrender my thoughts over the course of the next hour.

I pointed to the chair in the corner. "Can I use that one instead?"

"Sure, if that's what you'd like."

"Do you mind if I move it?"

"Actually, I got it." He walked over, effortlessly lifted the chair, and put it in front of *the chair.*

"Thank you, Dr. Blackwell." I sat and crossed my legs.

He did the same.

"So, what would you like to know?" I asked.

He flipped the pages of his notebook and put on his glasses. "Whatever you would like to discuss."

I scratched my head. "Well, I'm not quite sure how to answer that. Honestly, I'm not sure how I even feel about therapy. My ex-husband surely *was not* a fan."

He nodded and rubbed his chiseled jawline. "Mm-hmm, I see. So, am I your first?"

"Something like that."

He furrowed his brow before he nodded again and jotted something in his notepad. He uncrossed his legs, removed his glasses, and leaned forward as he studied me. "Hmm. Well, something obviously brought you here today. I'll tell you what. Since this is our first session, why don't you share whatever you're comfortable with."

Normally a stare that intense would've made me uncomfortable, but his eyes were kind. They reminded me of my daddy, and I immediately felt my walls begin to crumble. This was *my* moment. I needed this. I didn't need to be concerned with what my ex-husband or anyone else thought. This is why I was paying Dr. Leon the big bucks.

I took a deep breath before I began to spill my guts.

"So, some would say I have it all: a career I love, three beautiful daughters, several grandchildren, the freedom to live as I please. Even with all of that though, my life is a mess and I feel it's because of love. I feel like I'm losing in love … in every area of my life."

"What makes you say that?"

I took a deep breath and closed my eyes. "Well, Dr. Blackwell, I'm not your average fifty-three-year-old woman. I'm what these young kids would call *off the chain*. For years I tried to be the good girl and live up to my mom's and sister's expectations, but now I've become the rebel when it comes to my love life. Personally, I think whoever said growing older is supposed to make you wiser lied when it comes to love and relationships. I thought I had it all figured out at one point. At my age, I thought it would've gotten easier, but for me, it's been quite the opposite. I've done it all … a monogamous marriage, open relationships, swinging, you name it. I've probably done it."

He leaned back in his chair and crossed his legs again before putting his glasses back on. He wrote something in his notepad and said, "Well, when it comes to matters of the heart, I would like to think age doesn't always play a factor. We may grow and change in what we want, but love isn't usually cut and dry. Tell me this: would you consider yourself a polygamist?"

"Hmm, I wouldn't label myself anything. I just enjoy variety. A little flirting here, every now and then some sex there. Monogamy can get boring at times. You know? I just realized early on that it was a lot to ask for any person, particularly a man, to be with only one woman for the rest of their life. Wouldn't you agree?"

He paused as he contemplated what I'd just said. "I can't say that I agree completely. While it isn't easy for *men or women* to remain exclusive, it is quite possible."

I uncrossed my legs and recrossed them in the other direction. I looked at his finger, and there was no ring. *He probably doesn't have a clue.*

He followed my eyes. Before I could speak again, he continued. "And, to answer your question, yes, I've been married before. My *ex-wife* was the one who cheated. Several times, as a matter of fact."

My eyes widened at his admission. I opened my mouth to speak, but the only words I could find were "Oh. Okay."

"Yes, but back to you. You said earlier that you think your life is a mess because of love. What makes you say that?"

"Personally, I think I might be addicted to being in love. My drug of choice is love. I *love* love. At least I used to before my life started falling apart. The problem is, I'm horrible at it. I can't seem to get it right."

"Well, you're not alone. If it were easy, everyone would be in love."

I took a few deep breaths and shifted uncomfortably in my chair as I tried to avoid the emotions bubbling to the surface. "Yes, true, but now my past is haunting me."

He furrowed his brow. "Hmm ... okay. Is that why you said your life is a mess? Because of your past?"

"Most definitely. My life was much simpler until several months ago. Years ago, I left my husband because of an affair.

But now, I realize I'm still in love with my ex-husband, who I believe is the love of my life. I want him back, but now I may have also lost him too … for good this time. My sister and I are barely speaking, *and* someone is trying to destroy me. Things have just been … really messed up lately. The sad thing is, I've caused a lot of this on myself. I've hurt people without even realizing it."

Tears rimmed my eyes and Dr. Blackwell handed me a tissue.

"Well, coming to see me today is the first step. We're going to get through this. We'll take it one session at a time until we figure it out."

I nodded, dried my eyes, and straightened in the chair. "That sounds like a plan. But, since you're going to have to get all up in my business, let me properly introduce myself."

"Okay."

"To my children, I'm simply Iya. To my friends, I'm Amina. To the music world, I'm Amina 'Badass.' My name is Amina Thompkins, and I'm a Love Enthusiast."

# Music is Love

Five months earlier

Love is the drug I want coursing through my veins.
Love is the thing that keeps making me insane.
I can't leave it alone, though sometimes I want to.

But I'm under love's spell; it's like voodoo …

"Welcome to Blazin' 106.8, Miami's hottest morning show on your RAY-D-O! You've just heard Love's Addiction by Amina 'Badass.' Today, we'd like to welcome the *legendary* Amina 'Badass' to our show. We are so privileged to have her here today!" Jameson, one of the radio hosts, exclaimed.

I threw my head back and laughed along with Angel and Mel, the two other hosts of Blazin' 106.8 at Jameson's colorful presentation. This wasn't my first rodeo as far as interviews went. I had been in the music industry for many years but hadn't sat down to be interviewed in quite some time. I was a bit nervous before we got started because I was familiar with this show. These three were notorious for uncovering and sharing people's dirty little secrets, and I didn't want to be their next victim. God knew I had done my share of dirt. Thankfully, the hosts were making me feel at home.

"Thank you, Jameson. That was one *hell* of an introduction!" I added.

"Indeed, indeed! Nothing but the best for one of the best to ever do it! We can't wait to hear all about you! Your single is fiyah. I can't *wait* to hear the rest of the album! I'm so glad you're out here doing your thang again. What have you been up to for the past few years?"

"Well, I never go too far, but every now and then, I step away from the limelight to regroup. I never stop singing with my band though. Other than that, I've been traveling some and spending a lot of time with family. Especially my granddaughter."

They all gasped in unison.

"Grandkids! No way!" Angel exclaimed.

"Girl, you know good black don't crack, but I ain't no spring chicken. I'll be fifty-three next month. I have a two-year-old granddaughter and another on the way. Not quite sure what my daughter is having yet though. She's been pretty tight-lipped about it."

"Wow! If I can look half as good as you when I get to your age, I'll be happy," Mel said.

I grinned. "Well, thank you. Eating healthy and doing my yoga helps to keep me young."

"We see! So, tell us about your upcoming project," Jameson said.

A cheesy grin ran across my face when I thought about dropping another album. It had been years since I'd been in a studio. All the people who had slept on me in the past were about to find out that Amina 'Badass' didn't play when it came to her music. This time I had done a few collaborations with some of the young-ins in the industry.

I put my hand to my chest. "Yes, I feel extremely humbled to still be relevant after all these years. Several young artists reached out for collabs as well."

"What? That's pretty dope!" Jameson exclaimed.

"Right, I was surprised they knew my music like that. It definitely feels good."

"I know that's right! But your music appeals to every age, Ms. Amina. I grew up listening to your stuff," Angel said.

"Girl, just call me Amina. And, wow, that's amazing, Angel! I truly appreciate that. I never get tired of hearing that!"

"So, Amina. I have a question. What is something you'd like your fans to know about you?" Jameson asked.

"Hmm. Well, I'm not a *traditional celebrity*." I put my fingers up in air quotes to emphasize the words. "In fact, I wouldn't say I'm traditional at all. For the most part, I'm not big on being in the limelight. I drive myself most of the time, I do my own shopping, I still live in my condo, I don't live extravagantly. I'm not interested in all the pomp and circumstance."

"Well, I sure can't tell. You surely *look* like a million bucks," Mel said.

I smiled and moved one of my dreadlocks from my face. "Thank you, Mel," I said and blew a few kisses in his direction.

"So, what about your love life, Amina? I'm sure a beautiful woman like yourself has plenty of suitors," Mel asked. He smiled slyly at me before looking me up and down, licking his lips.

I had to admit, I was a sucker for a fine man, and he was definitely that. I didn't usually go for the pretty boys, but I wouldn't have minded running my fingers through his full head of curls and kissing on his smooth brown skin. I was also tempted to lick that dimple on his left cheek. It didn't help that his shirt was fitted, so I could see how defined his chest was as he flexed his muscular arms and flirted with me.

It was amazing how bold these young men were today. Instead of being appalled, though, I was flattered. He didn't know who he was dealing with. I had conquered many from the young to the old, but I chose to keep my love life private. I always kept non-disclosure agreements close and wasn't afraid to whip one out if need be. If this was a few years ago, Mel and I probably would've gotten it on right after the show wrapped for the day.

I smiled coyly. "Uh-uh-uh … you sly devil, you. Now, you know that's where I draw the line. I don't like to talk about my love life. But I will give you this: I play by a different set of rules when it comes to love and relationships. I've learned that I don't do well with love when I try to do it by societal norms. That's why I never remarried after my first husband."

"Oh *really*. Why is that?" Angel asked.

I frowned when Malcolm's face popped into my mind. He was the first man I fell in love with and wanted to marry. Unfortunately, he had other plans. Then, I smiled when I pictured my ex-husband: the love of my life, the man I couldn't seem to get over. Unfortunately, we also couldn't seem to get it together. Finally, my daddy and first love. He cheated on my mother during their marriage too. No man could ever be faithful, as far as I was concerned. Period, point blank. That was my truth.

"Well, I would say my view of relationships changed when I was around seventeen. I had a relationship that didn't go the way I thought it would, so it made me begin to see things differently. Let's just say the failure of that relationship opened my mind to new things."

Angel nodded. "Very interesting. But most people experience heartbreak, and they still believe in good ole love and marriage the old-fashioned way. I'm one of those people."

I nodded.

"I hear you, but I'm non-conventional and I do believe love is one of those things where one size doesn't fit all. Everyone chooses to love in the way that's best fit for them. Don't get me wrong. I *love* love. I sing about love, I dream about love, I always want to be in love. It isn't perfect. It's unpredictable and carries a lot of heartbreak. Although I still haven't figured out how to navigate love's impetuous waters, I still crave it. I still desire to ride the waves of emotion that love can cause. There's nothing better than that four-letter word for me. I mean, who wouldn't want that feeling of euphoria that comes when another person wants to share their world with you?"

Jameson and Angel leaned forward as they hung on to my every word.

"That's so deep, Amina," Jameson said, googly-eyed.

"But why keep your love life a secret if you admire love so much?" Mel asked. He pulled his sunglasses down and peered over them at me. "Unless you have some skeletons in that closet."

Angel and Jameson held their breath and stared at me as they awaited my response.

I smirked at Mel's attempt to corner me into admission. Everyone had something they'd prefer not to share. I was no different. "Let's just say I've enjoyed life's journey in love."

The rest of the interview went well, with no more prodding questions about my love life. As soon as it ended, Mel leaned in and handed me his card.

"What's this for?" I asked.

He looked me up and down. "I'd like to take you for dinner sometime. You know I like 'em a little older. That's *if* you think you can handle a young man like myself."

I smirked. "Oh, I can more than handle you, young brotha. How old are you anyway?"

"I'll be thirty-eight in a few weeks."

I leaned forward just enough for him to see what I was working with. He was practically drooling.

I imagined him naked. Oh, the possibilities. But I could barely keep up with what I had going on in my own relationship at the moment. I shook it off and stood up abruptly.

"The offer is tempting, but I'll pass. Enjoy the rest of your day."

With that, I turned on my heels and made my way out the door.

# Still in Love

"Umph, umph, umph," Khalil said as we emerged out of our daughter Anisa's home. "Damn, baby, you still got it."

I heard what he said but refused to acknowledge his comment. I had rushed over to console my daughter after hearing her voice on our call not too long before. Other than my career, my girls were my life. She was scaring me, and there was nothing I wouldn't do for my children. When I heard the pain in her voice, I knew something was off, so I threw on some clothes, dialed her father while I was in the car, and picked him up on my way to her house since he was on the way.

I could tell something was off when she had bailed on my show the night before, claiming she wasn't feeling well. I figured she was hiding something, but I didn't let on. When

I called to check on her today, she couldn't hide her emotions anymore. It broke my heart when she said, "I'm so sorry."

"Oh my goodness! Sorry for what? Are you okay, queen?" I asked.

"No," she cried.

"Oh my God! What's wrong?" I asked.

"I'm a horrible person and an even worse daughter," she said.

She was scaring me, and I panicked. "What are you talking about? Do you need me to come over?"

"N-n-no."

Her answer wasn't good enough. I needed to go and see her in person to make sure she was okay.

"Okay. I'm coming now. See you in a minute," I said and hung up. I dialed Khalil, who promptly agreed to go with me. I knew she wouldn't be expecting him, but I wanted him there, even though we tended to handle things differently as parents. He was a bit uncouth at times and always wanted to put his hands on someone. While we rode to her house, I said, "I think it might be something with her and her boyfriend."

"Did she say that?" he asked.

I shrugged. "No, it's just a hunch, but I know my daughter."

He balled his fists up. "If he put his hands on her …"

"Let's just see what happened before you get all bent out of shape," I urged.

He nodded and clenched his jaw. For Terrence's sake—he was Anisa's boyfriend—I hoped he hadn't touched my daughter either.

When Anisa opened the door and I saw her tear-stained face, I couldn't do anything more than wrap my arms around her tightly as her tears were unleashed.

As soon as we made it into the house, I asked, "What's going on, queen?"

Khalil was ready. The first thing he said was, "What the hell did that man do to my baby?"

I shook my head. *Here we go.*

She rubbed her swollen eyes and said, "Daddy, I'm okay."

"You don't look okay," he said. "What, have you been lying around here crying all day?"

"Sort of."

"Well, it's time to get back up now. You know better than to let this punk keep you down," he said. He wasn't giving her a chance to breathe.

I frowned. "Khalil, give my child a break!"

"She's my child too."

Typical man. So insensitive. I narrowed my eyes at him to let him know I wasn't playing.

He backed down and went into the kitchen. "You have something to drink?" he yelled.

"Yes," Anisa squeaked. "I have plenty of juice in the fridge and plenty of water and sodas in the pantry."

I rolled my eyes and yelled for him to stop bothering her.

When he came back out, he said, "So, tell us what happened."

Thankfully, Anisa didn't say he had hurt her physically. In fact, it was the other way around. Anisa was the one who had put her hands on Terrence. She repeated what Terrence had said to her when she told him to get out: "Look at you. No one is ever going to want you."

I cringed when I heard Terrence's words and was secretly happy at her reaction, but I didn't let on. Especially with Khalil present. Anisa's boyfriend must've really done a number on her for her to punch him.

Khalil didn't hide his satisfaction about her using what he had taught our daughters for self-defense, though. He said, "That's my baby. I'm glad that you handled your business. I see you put my how-to-knock-a-fool-out-in-three-moves class to use."

I rubbed my temples and glared at him. "What if he had hit her back? You know I don't promote violence."

His reply: "I wish he would've. That's the last thing he would've done."

I rubbed my eyes and focused my attention back on my daughter. "Do you need me to stay here with you tonight?"

"Amina, stop babying that woman. She's grown," Khalil fussed.

I opened my mouth to answer, but Anisa interjected. "I'm okay. Really. I just needed a minute to get it all out, but I'm fine. I really am."

"You sure?" I asked.

She nodded and smiled at me. I wasn't sure how truthful she was being, but this time I decided to take Khalil's advice and stop babying her. "Okay, queen, but if you need me, you just pick up the phone," I said before I kissed her cheek.

Her father hugged her but couldn't help himself. He attempted to whisper, but I heard him loud and clear. "Remember what I said. Don't let anyone steal your shine, beautiful, and good job with his eye. I knew you had it in you."

"Khalil!" I yelled.

He obediently followed me out the door.

Now I was rolling my eyes at Khalil as we exited Anisa's house, refusing to acknowledge his comment that I had "still got it." I kept making my way to my destination.

When we got to the car, I shook my head and side-eyed my ex-husband. "Why would you tell her you were proud of her for putting hands on that man? You know I taught them better than that."

He gave a sly grin, and while I wanted to stay upset with him, my heart fluttered.

"You're so beautiful when you're upset. You know that?" he said, completely ignoring my comment. "Besides, he don't want none of this." He opened my car door and I got in. I craned my neck to watch him as his bowlegs carried him to the passenger's side.

The older he got, the sexier he became. When he smiled, his eyes held the slightest crinkle in the corners, and the hair on his temples was gray, which made him look like a distinguished gentleman and even sexier to me. Typical Khalil saying and doing what he pleased even though he knew I was with someone else. Who could blame him, considering the way our relationship ended? I guess me being in an open relationship didn't help either because no matter what I said, he didn't believe open relationships could be real.

I glanced over at him as I started the car. I had loved this man more than life itself at one point. Hell, I still wasn't over him, and I didn't know if I would ever be. He was the only man who could convince me to get married and have children, and even though I never thought I wanted kids, I was glad he had convinced me otherwise. While marriage may have been a mistake, my daughters were one of my proudest accomplishments.

"Khalil, what you taught them is for self-defense, and that man *did not* put his hands on her. How can you even begin to think that's okay?"

He sighed and leaned back in the seat. "Amina, you know that joke of a man she has is not good for her. Damn shame she's been with him this long, and I've seen him what—" He paused, raised his pointer finger, and looked over at me. "Maybe once? I'm sure she felt the need to do what she had to if she put hands on him."

I shook my head and blew out air. There was no reasoning with this man … I'd never met someone so damn hardheaded. I went to open my mouth as I wanted to reach over and shake some sense into him, but as I did, my phone rang. Adebayo's name flashed across the screen.

"Hey, honey," I answered without looking over at Khalil. I put my Bluetooth device in my ear and looked back as I slowly proceeded out of the driveway.

"*Hey, honey,*" Khalil repeated in mock fashion. Out of the corner of my eye, I saw him wave me off.

I chuckled. It was no secret how he felt about Adebayo. It had been this way with us for years. Me constantly dodging his advances, and him enjoying how uncomfortable it made me. Khalil's favorite thing to say was "If you can sleep with other men, why can't I be one of them? Your man shouldn't care."

I would roll my eyes. "Khalil, yes, we are polyamorous, but we have rules. While Adebayo and I have an open relationship, it doesn't mean we can just sleep with anyone. You are a *definite* no on the list."

As I said those words, I had to question if that was still the case with my partner and bandmate. My relationship with Adebayo was now taking another course. I wouldn't dare let Khalil know that though.

Adebayo and I had the no-exes rule for a reason. Well, the no-exes part was actually his idea. I think he saw there was still plenty of love between Khalil and I, and he didn't want to risk losing me to the man he took me from. It sounded ridiculous, but what Khalil and I had didn't come along often, and Adebayo knew if I went back in that direction, I might never leave—or maybe that was my guilt on how my relationship with Adebayo had begun.

I had met Khalil at one of my gigs in a local restaurant in the Miami area, and we hit it off immediately. He walked in the joint oozing a confidence and sex appeal that I wasn't used to, and I was immediately smitten. In fact, I was so taken off guard that I missed my cue to come in when the band started playing. I cleared my throat and looked back at my drummer, giving the sign for him to stop playing—which was a no no. As I was taught in this live music world, when you mess up, you don't start over. You simply adjust and continue. Thank goodness my amazing band members didn't flinch. My drummer gave his count again and tapped his drum. This time, I was able to do what I came to do. I opened my mouth, and the melodic sounds were unleashed.

My nineteen-year-old self was smitten as I watched the sexy stranger's eyes widen. He gave his full attention to my performance as he leaned against the bar and sipped his drink. Like many, he was probably shocked that such a big sound could come from my little body. Little did he know, I came from a long line of gospel and soul singers.

He continued to stare as I added a few extra runs in the song to show off my skills. I closed my eyes and did what I did best. I let the music move through my body and soul as only music could.

He was a hunk of a man, tall and ruggedly handsome with a little edge, just the way I liked 'em. And those bowlegs, bay bay! I didn't have a chance! His body was also lean and toned, so I figured he worked out, which was perfect. *Maybe we could go running together*, I thought. *Then, when we get back from our run, I'll take him for a test run in the sheets.* As I imagined which position I wanted him to put me in first, an attractive woman appeared and threw her arms around his neck. She kissed his cheek and threw her head back as she laughed, hard enough for me to see all her dental work. He held his arm out and *Ms. Thang* looped her tired arm through it.

*Oh no he didn't.* I couldn't believe he was there with a woman after he just eye-fucked me. Typical.

I did my best to divert my attention from him and his hussy, but it was too late. He already had me, and without saying a word, I finished my set and walked away from the stage area. I put a little extra twist in my hips as I walked around the room to greet the patrons and thank them for coming out. I momentarily debated if I should bypass his table because I didn't want to see him with her, but I said fuck it. This was my world, and she was just a nut.

I went over to their table last and batted my eyes at him as I spoke. "Well, I've never seen you here before."

She cleared her throat. I glanced in her direction and gave her a plastic grin. "Oh, my mistake. I've never seen *any* of you here before." I focused my attention back on him and asked, "So, are you enjoying the show?"

He shifted in his chair uncomfortably. "Umm, yes, the band is amazing—and your voice is angelic."

He jumped slightly and I realized she had most likely kicked him under the table. He focused his attention back on her, grabbed her hand, and tucked it under his arm. "This is my girlfriend, Sydney."

*Sydney, huh? Hmm. Only a girlfriend?*

She reached her other hand out, for a handshake. "How do you do?"

I grabbed her fingers ever so slightly and shook her hand. "I'm awesome." I focused my attention back on him and grinned again. I rested my hand on his shoulder and said, "I hope to see you again."

Before he could respond, she squinted and spoke. "Oh yes, *we* would love to come out again."

I looked over at her. *Oh, it will only be a matter of time before he'll be mine, so enjoy him while you can.*

I smiled ever so sweetly and said, "Great, I look forward to it." With that, I spun on my heels and sashayed away from their table. I went back to the stage and took my place as the band resumed our set. I closed my eyes and showed out some more. When I opened them, Khalil's eyes were boring a hole into me. We locked gazes as his eyes glazed over while he took in my performance. I knew he was hooked.

*Got you*, I thought as I worked the stage as I had never done before. Hell, they didn't call me Amina 'Badass' for nothing …

I swerved slightly on the road.

"Whoa, Amina, what the fuck!" Khalil yelled, jolting me back to present day reality.

I blinked a few times and slowed down. "Shoot! My apologies, I got distracted."

"You need me to drive?" he asked as he glanced between me and the road.

"I got it, I got it," I replied, like I hadn't almost killed us a few short moments before.

# Jealousy and Love

When I got to the house, I spotted Zion's car in the driveway—Zion was Adebayo's son. I was glad to see he was here because maybe Adebayo would lay off me some. When I went inside, Adebayo greeted me at the door in his normal fashion. He bowed his head and lowered his eyes, saying, "My queen."

His dreads, which I adored, had been recently cut into a mohawk. I was getting used to this look on him.

I mirrored his actions, saying, "My king."

I kicked my shoes off—to leave the germs and the negative spirits outside—and put my bag down by the door. He was brewing tea as he normally did. The house smelled of mint and garlic. No doubt he was probably sampling another one of his concoctions.

Zion wasn't far behind. He walked over to me and kissed me on the cheek. The hair from his beard tickled my face. He was a smidgen taller, but I swear, that young man looked just like his father, down to the mohawk he wore. The only difference was his hair was dyed blond.

"Hello, Miss Amina," he said and smiled at me.

"Hello, young king," I answered and smiled back. "And it's *just* Amina. We don't need all the formalities. Leaving so soon? You know you're welcome to stay for dinner."

"Yes, Miss—I mean, Amina. I appreciate that, but I just came by to drop something off with Dad. I'll be back around soon enough though."

I smiled, playfully pointed, and said, "Okay now. You make sure to do that."

"Yes, ma'am!" Zion said as he walked out the door, and as expected, it didn't take long for Adebayo to lay into me.

He followed me to the kitchen. "So, my queen ..." He paused. I knew what was coming next. "Who were you with earlier today?"

As suspected, he'd heard Khalil's voice in the background when I was leaving my daughter's house. I did my best not to roll my eyes as I debated if I should tell him where I just came from. Music was the only thing we seemed to agree on these days, so I attempted to steer him in that direction. "I wrote some amazing lyrics today."

He nodded, but I could tell my attempt at distracting him wasn't working.

I leaned against the sink as I made one more futile attempt to move away from the upcoming conversation I didn't want to have. "Oh, remember I have those workmen coming next week, and I won't be here, so make sure you're here to let them in."

He sat at the kitchen table and stared at me. He nodded. "Yes, I remember."

I paused and chose my next words carefully. "And I just came from Anisa's house. She sounded rough on the phone, so I rushed over."

His eyes grew wide. In that moment, he seemed genuinely concerned. "Oh, is she okay?"

"Yes. I think she'll be fine."

"Okay, good!" he paused. I clenched my butt cheeks and waited for it. He wasn't done. "Did you go alone?"

Our relationship was getting exhausting. I never expected to be here with him like this. Adebayo was acting like a jealous boyfriend.

*Dammit.* Although I didn't believe in telling lies, this was where I could easily tell a little one. "No, not exactly."

He sighed again and worry lines creased his forehead. "I would've gone with you."

I side-eyed him and gritted my teeth. I didn't want to hurt his feelings, so I searched my mind for the best way to respond. I took a deep breath. "I appreciate that, Bayo … but you're not her father."

He shook his head and diverted his eyes. He spoke so low, I had to strain to hear him. "You know, for someone you're no longer with, you sure have been spending a lot of time together lately."

I closed my eyes, leaned my head in my palms, and took a deep breath. It was no use trying to explain myself to him. He would always be jealous of my ex-husband no matter how hard I tried. Maybe it was the undeniable chemistry Khalil and I would always have, or maybe it was just his insecurities. Whatever it was, I wouldn't dare tell him he was right.

Adebayo and I had an arrangement. We both had our own places (my rule) because I wanted us to always have our own space, even though we enjoyed most of our time together. Some weeks, I'd stay at his place and vice versa. Our situation worked well for both of us ... at first. He claimed he was happy with our arrangement, and I don't know if it was just my imagination or what, but lately, it felt as if he was getting clingy.

I washed my hands, grabbed a mug, and poured some tea. Then I sat at the table beside him. "So, did you look for any gigs today?" I asked.

"Not really."

I took a sip. "And why is that?"

He shrugged. "Didn't really feel like it. I'll work on it tomorrow."

I sighed as I contemplated the best way to get my point across. Realizing there was no good way, I pushed forward. "My king, I need you to find a life outside of ours. I've been urging you to look for other bands to play for as well because our working *and* sleeping together is beginning to be a bit much. Don't you feel ... smothered?"

He winced and his shoulders slumped. I knew my words were harsh. "Oh, wow. Well … no … I don't. Actually, I *love* being in your company."

"Oh." His answer surprised me. I felt like the Wicked Witch of the South.

He reached over and grabbed my hand. "I love you so much, but something has to give. I don't know if I can keep going like this."

"Going like what? Things are fine on my end."

"And that's just it. *Your* end. I'm just saying, we've been doing this open relationship thing for quite some time now and maybe we should consider slowing down. When I found you, I found everything I wanted and needed. I love only you, and frankly, my dick is tired. You're probably the only woman that could have me thinking about getting remarried again. Besides, there's only so much fuckin' and hanging out a man can do."

Truthfully, I couldn't understand what his issue was. Most men would *kill* to be in his shoes: having a woman not breathing down your neck, or letting you enjoy other women. But here he was, messing up the game plan. At this point, it was rare that we even dated other people, and I did it for him, but still, monogamy wasn't on my radar.

Suddenly, I felt hot. My body became damp with perspiration. That's what happened any time someone referenced me and marriage in the same sentence. I sprang up from my seat. I wasn't sure if it was a hot flash or Adebayo's words, but I didn't want to hear it.

"I need some water." I grabbed a glass out of the cabinet, went to the sink, and turned on the faucet. My reaction didn't cause him to slow down though.

"And another thing. Have you thought about what we spoke about before regarding your last name?"

Several months before, he had asked about me possibly changing my last name back to my maiden name, but I dismissed it because I thought he was talking out the side of his neck. He wasn't making sense. Other than his jealousy for Khalil, he couldn't give me a good reason for changing my last name.

"I told you that wasn't an option, Bayo."

"But you were already a star before you got married, and you can't use your girls as an excuse anymore as to why you're keeping his last name. Nia and Talia are married, so their last names have changed, and I figure one day Anisa will be married too."

I took a few more sips of my water and allowed my mind to drift off. I wasn't trying to argue. He was correct with me hanging on to my marital name for more than my girls. I wasn't ready to let Khalil go altogether. Keeping his name kept me bonded to him in my own strange way.

"Amina, did you hear what I was saying?" he asked.

I blinked myself back into reality. "What's that?"

Adebayo got up and came over to me. Without breaking eye contact, he took my glass from my hands and rested it on the counter. "I was saying, I love you, woman, and I want us to work. Let's figure out how to do this."

I nodded. "I love you too."

He leaned in. I threw my arms around his neck and planted my lips on his. When our lips touched, my body melded with his. We were two peas in a pod when it came to the bedroom.

He effortlessly lifted me off my feet without us breaking our kiss. We'd barely made it to the bedroom when I began tearing his shirt off his body. I kissed his neck and shoulders. He pulled my dress down at the neck and found his way to one of my breasts. Before I knew it, it was in his mouth.

I felt my body go weak as he gently licked then bit my nipple until I moaned. I knew what kind of sex session this would be. This was what we did whenever there was tension between us. This was how we resolved our issues. This was how we made up, how we loved. This was how he managed to make me lower my inhibitions. He put me up against the wall and entered me as I gritted my teeth and put my hands in his mohawk. I threw my head back as he grinded into me. When I thought I couldn't take it anymore, he put me down and bent me over the bed.

He entered me from behind. He grabbed my waist as he pounded into me. It hurt so good. I pushed my ass in the air to give him better access and matched his hip movements. The clapping of skin against skin, our moans, and the banging of the headboard were the only sounds in the house. When I thought I couldn't take it anymore, he pulled out. He didn't have to say a word.

I flipped onto my back, and we continued our session. When I couldn't take it anymore, I cried out, "I'm coming!"

He closed his eyes and went harder. He kept grinding into me until our bodies were soaked in my juices. By the time we were done, my body was so spent, I forgot what I had been concerned with just a few moments before.

Sexually, he was everything to me that my ex-husband was not. For now, he wouldn't have to worry about me going anywhere.

# Family is Love

As I was consulting my new vegan cookbook for a new dish, the name *Jackie* flashed across my phone's screen.

I rolled my eyes and plastered on a fake smile before I answered the call. "Hey, sis," I sang.

"Hey, little sis. What have you been up to today?"

"Same ole, same ole."

"When is the last time you spoke to Mom? She's been fussing about you never calling her. Says you just threw her away."

As usual, she couldn't wait to start something with me. I loved my sister, but I didn't want to hear any negativity, and she always found a way to rain on my damn parade. I rolled my eyes when she mentioned our mother. Other than my sister, she was the only other person I rarely wanted to speak to.

My mother always thought there was something wrong

with me. For as long as I could remember, singing was the only thing I wanted to do, and she thought I was foolish for aspiring to be a songstress. She would compare me and my older sister all the time—she couldn't understand why I didn't want to have a good ole *regular career*. In fact, she couldn't understand how we were so different. My mother's constant comparisons were overwhelming. Jackie's buttoned-down lifestyle of being an educator was applauded. Damn the fact I had gotten many awards and a host of loyal fans from what I did.

Memories of being called the "black sheep" still annoyed me, and to this day, I still sometimes questioned if I was good enough. In a time when being a dark-skinned Black girl was already a struggle, I needed my mother's approval. My light-skinned all-honors-student sister was her favorite.

My anxiety grew as I thought about my childhood, so I decided to switch subjects.

"Jackie, do you need something? I don't feel like talking about Mom today."

"You never do, but okay. It would just be nice if you'd go and see her sometimes. I'm *not* an only child, you know," she huffed.

It never felt that way to me anymore, but I wouldn't dare mention it. I knew it wouldn't be enough to placate her, but I answered, "I just sent you money to get someone to stay in the house with her."

She puffed out air. I could tell she was frustrated.

"Whatever, Amina. Money can't replace your time, but of course I'm preaching to the choir."

We both sighed as tense energy rose through the phone.

"Anyways, I was just checking to see if you were still coming to Kareem's graduation next week. I need a count since there's only a handful of tickets."

I smiled when I thought of my nephew. Having him was one of the things my sister had gotten right. "Of course. I'm overjoyed that my nephew will be going to grad school shortly. I still can't believe it … Time's flying! So proud of him!"

I could hear her grinning through the phone when she spoke. "Me too! I just wish I could do something more for him than dinner. He deserves so much more."

I shook my head. She was right about him being deserving, but she forgot it was partially her fault she couldn't give him what he deserved. The money she should've been saving for his education after her last divorce was used to splurge on handbags, clothes, and non-essential items. She ran through her ex-husband's money like Usain Bolt ran through the Olympics. That's another reason I was so frugal now.

"And, just so you know, Mom *will* be there, so I hope you can at least *try* to speak before then. How long has it been again?"

Her insistence on bringing up my mom was grating on my nerves. As usual, she was ignoring my feelings and injecting her will on me. Figures, she was always on Mom's side.

"You really need to think about the way you live your life,

Amina. The way you've lived your life, and the things your girls have seen, has caused them to make very unfavorable decisions regarding their love lives. Besides, don't you think you're getting a little too old for this lifestyle?"

I rolled my eyes again and wrinkled my brow as I knew what she was going to say next, but I decided to ask anyway. "And what would 'this lifestyle' be, Mrs. Perfect?"

"You know … the open relationships, and the inability to commit to one person."

I sighed. I didn't plan to explain myself to her. She would never understand how watching the way she and Mom lived their lives made me want to live mine differently. They had played a huge part in the way I chose to love. Especially with her being divorced three times, my mother and father arguing all the time, and our parents separating before Dad passed away.

My sister stayed with her head shoved so far up my mother's ass, she couldn't see anything else.

I decided to switch topics and turn the tables back on her before this conversation went to the point of no return. "So, since you're asking about Mom, when is the last time you went to visit Dad's grave?"

She sighed and the line went silent. You could cut the tension with a knife. She felt about him the way I felt about my mother. "I haven't been since we talked about me going the last time."

I wasn't surprised, but I gasped to make my point. "Jackie,

now you know you need to do better!" I mused. She began to fuss as I heard my other line beep. "I need to take this. You mind if I call you back?"

The dial tone was my answer.

Before I went to bed that night, I headed to the safe in my closet. Speaking to Jackie and thinking about her inability to give my nephew the things he wanted were my motivation to make sure I always stacked my paper. I always kept several thousand dollars in there to cover any emergencies I might have. I wasn't too fond of most banking institutions, so I would deposit just enough money to cover my bills on a monthly basis.

Even so, Adebayo and I had a small account together at the bank that we both contributed to. Like Jackie, he wasn't good with his money, so he gave me his portion to manage. I also had the checkbook and debit card for him from that account safely tucked away in the safe. My daughters were the only ones who knew the lock code besides me. In the event of my early demise, they could access my passwords along with directions on what they could do with the money in the bank accounts, as well as my obituary in the safe.

I had just added a few dollars to the safe to replace what I had borrowed recently when I was startled by Adebayo's voice behind me.

"That's my queen. Always on point with that money. I know you're non-conventional and all, but don't you think it's time to find a better way to store money?"

I put my hand to my chest. "Oh my goodness, Bayo, I

told you about sneaking up behind me! You almost gave me a heart attack."

He kissed the back of my neck and wrapped his arms around my waist. "Sorry, queen. I didn't mean to startle you. I was just wondering if you wanted to find a better way to store money and whatnot, and I'm thinking you might want to invest in security cameras. Your alarm system is good, but a woman in your position should consider having more security."

I nodded at his observation. Maybe he was right, but as the saying goes, *if it ain't broke, don't fix it.* "This system has been working fine for me for years now, so I think I'll leave well enough alone, but you can let me know if you're ready for your card and account information from our joint account. I'll be glad to give it to you."

He nodded. "I know, I know. I like the way you handle our account *and* other things too. If you know what I mean." He let me go and grinned at me slyly. "I'm waiting for you, baby," he said before walking out of the closet.

I grinned from ear to ear because I knew what time it was.

"Oh, I'll be right there, my king." I closed the safe and followed him to the bedroom. I had so much pent-up frustration from speaking to my sister earlier, and I was ready to work it off with my man.

# Friendship and Love

My ride-or-die bestie, Joy, and I met up the next evening for dinner. My girl was always down for a glass or two now that her divorce was almost final and she'd finally managed to usher the last of her two children out of the house. Like me, Joy was always a good time.

My favorite thing about her was that she never judged me. She might not have understood me all the time, but she always supported what would make me happy, no matter how extreme it seemed. Hence, my love life … She was the only other person who knew all of what had gone down with Khalil and my affair with Adebayo. She was also the only person who knew that I was still very much in love with Khalil.

She was a ball of energy, and although she had me by a few years in the age department, she looked at least ten years younger.

Joy's bubbly personality entered the room before she did.

When she spotted me sitting by the bar, her walk quickly matched the music and she danced her way right over to where I was. There was no way to stay sad or upset around this woman, and I couldn't help but fall out with laughter when I saw her moves.

"Hey, friend!" she yelled a little louder than necessary over the music. By the way she was acting, I wasn't sure if she had already started drinking, but I didn't care. She needed to take a few more back with her girl.

I returned her excitement, hugged her tightly, and stepped back. "Hey, girl! You're looking good!"

"Thank you!" she answered, doing a quick spin to show how well her tight-ass dress hugged every curve.

We sat down to take in the ambiance, and she didn't waste time catching me up. "Girl, this divorce shit is for the birds! Every day, it seems as if there's some new stuff I didn't know could be done to me. You would think we never even liked each other by the tricks he's trying to pull."

"What happened now?" I asked.

"This fool is now asking for half of my money. The money *I* worked for *before* he even came into the picture. I couldn't help that he was doing nothing when I was up late at night working on getting *my* degree while he was out with his tricks. He's trying to take half of my savings, bitcoin, retirement, and anything else he can get his hands on. Can you believe that shit?"

I shook my head.

I felt for her. I hated that she was going through all of this. Thankfully, I had dodged that bullet with my ex-husband.

Only God knows what I would've done if Khalil had done that to me. I don't think we would've been able to have the relationship we did if he had tried to come after me like that. "Dang, my friend, that's messed up. Can he even do that?"

"I don't know, but I'm going to die trying to make sure he doesn't."

"Is there anything I can do to help?"

"Hmm. Maybe you can find someone to cut his brakes." She laughed.

My eyes grew wide. Although she laughed it off, there was no doubt that deep inside she really felt that way. "I hear you, girl. Thankfully, I didn't have to deal with those issues with Khalil, and I see men going through that all the time. That's another reason I don't know if I could ever get married again. I may not get so lucky the next time. Hell, even without all that drama, divorce almost broke me mentally."

She nodded. "That's because y'all had *no business* getting divorced in the first place. If I had what you had, I would've figured it out. You two were the original Michelle and Barack Obama … two peas in a pod."

I smiled.

She was partially correct. We were good together, until we weren't.

I went to respond but was quickly distracted when I heard laughter and a familiar voice coming from the other side of the room. *What are the chances?*

My nightmare was confirmed when I glanced over Joy's

shoulder and spotted my ex-husband with the one woman I never thought I'd see him with again.

Joy stopped talking mid-sentence and stared at me. "You okay?"

I didn't respond but threw my chin up toward the objects of my distraction.

Her eyes followed and widened when she spotted them. She mused, "Oh shoot. Look at Khalil getting his mack on." When I didn't respond or crack a smile, she glanced back at the couple. "Wait, you're not *jealous*, are you?" She smirked. "*Especially* when that man has been trying to get back with you for years, and you won't give him no play."

I shouldn't have been upset because I had already moved on. At least, I t*hought* I had. But my main problem was not that he was there with *a* woman—it was *the* woman he was with.

I leaned over and whispered, "Look at the woman, Joy!"

She scrunched her nose up in confusion and glanced back at them again. It didn't take long before the recognition hit. "Oh! Is that … ?"

"Yes! It is."

I watched as the woman playfully put her hand on his arm, threw her head back, and laughed out loud. That was her signature move. I remembered it vividly from over thirty years before. She looked the same, other than a few gray hairs. That pissed me off even more.

Joy didn't help when she whispered, "She looks *really* good." And I couldn't argue. Sydney, Khalil's ex, looked damn good. Of course, not better than me though. Thank goodness for Pilates and yoga.

"I should go over there," I answered without making eye contact with my friend.

Joy wasn't trying to hear it. "Don't you dare!" she said. My friend was ride-or-die, but she also believed in right and wrong. She knew my going over to Khalil and Sydney could cause no good.

I was usually non-confrontational, and I couldn't remember the last time I fought, but when it came to Khalil, I didn't know how far I would go.

I wiped my mouth with my napkin and got up from the table. Joy called my name, but I didn't stop. I wasn't going to cause any trouble, but I did want to let Khalil and his chick see how good I looked from the back when I walked away. But first, I wanted him to see that I saw him.

I stopped briefly at the table. "Well, hello Khalil."

He was obviously shocked to see me as well because he froze with his mouth open when we made eye contact. I found it funny that I still had that effect on him after all those years.

Sydney smirked at our exchange but attempted to play it off. "Hello, Amina. It's been ... a really long time."

I quickly became The Queen of Petty. "It has been a while, hasn't it?"

"You're looking ... good," she added.

I wouldn't dare repay the compliment. "Thank you."

She was handling seeing me better than I was seeing her.

In all actuality, I knew I had no business feeling this way, but because they were playing kissing games during our marriage, I always felt she stayed present in his heart.

Joy appeared behind me and gently touched my back. It was her subtle way of letting me know it was time to go. She handed me my bag. "Hello Khalil, hello Sydney. It's good to see you both."

Khalil finally broke out of his trance long enough to respond. "It's good seeing you as well, Joy."

Khalil and I stared at each other. It felt as though my feet were stuck in place.

Although I was too grown for these games, I couldn't help myself. I wasn't done being mischievous. Before walking out the door, I smirked and said, "I'll call you later, Khalil. We have some things to discuss regarding *our* children."

I caught a glimpse of Sydney rolling her eyes.

Joy plastered on a smile and wiggled her five fingers before grabbing my arm and pulling me toward the door. "Good night, y'all!" she yelled over her shoulder.

We didn't make it fully outside before she was on me. "What was all of that about?"

I paced back and forth in the parking lot. "He could've picked anyone else. Why her?"

Joy looked flustered. She took a deep breath. "Did you not see the way that man looked at you tonight? He's still in love with you. For God's sake, why don't you just be with him already?"

I was flustered. I threw my hands up and paced some

more. I couldn't understand why no one got my apprehension. She was my best friend and had been there from the beginning. If anyone should have understood, she should have.

"Joy, we already didn't work out the first time. Who's to say this time would be different? Plus, I love Bayo," I whined.

"Do you love Adebayo, or are you *in* love with him?"

I stopped pacing long enough to think about her question. Adebayo was a wonderful man, he was a safe choice, and he loved me. Why I couldn't just calm down and be with him was beyond me.

When I didn't answer, Joy rolled her eyes. "Girl, you're making my head spin. You have not one but *two* men in love with you. Poor Amina."

# When Love Comes A'knockin'

When I got home from dinner, I headed straight for the kitchen and poured myself a glass of wine. But instead of sipping it, I gulped it down as I pictured Khalil and Sydney sitting across the table from each other earlier on. It didn't feel good. It shouldn't have bothered me since I had *supposedly* moved on with Adebayo, but it did.

I got into bed, pulled the comforter over my head, closed my eyes, and attempted to fall asleep. I kicked the covers off though, and stared at the ceiling when I realized there was no sleep to be found. Lying here like this gave me déjà vu, and memories of what had happened so many years before plagued me.

My body stiffened as I remembered that fateful night.

I had come home early off the road from touring with the band. I wanted to surprise Khalil, but I was the one who was surprised when I saw him and Sydney embraced in a passionate kiss. The cab pulled up, and they were too caught up in each other to notice me. The passion I saw between the two of them had done something to me. It reminded me why I had sworn off marriage and began seeking open relationships in the first place. I trusted him when he said it would only be the two of us. But, like Malcolm, he had lied to me.

My legs shook as I got out of the cab and stood watching their interaction for a moment before I closed the cab door. The slamming door startled them. I wanted to run. Run just like I did with Malcolm. But with him, it was different. We had a family. I loved him too much to just give up on everything we had built together.

So, I forgave him when he said it was a mistake and it would never happen again. For all intents and purposes, he kept his end of the bargain. But, what he wasn't delivering was better sex.

Months later, like clockwork, I stared at the ceiling as Khalil's body grinded into mine.

"Let's try it this way," I suggested as I attempted to move him so I could turn over.

"I'm almost there, baby," he said.

I continued to stare at the ceiling as he grunted.

"Oh yeah. This is it, baby. I'm coming."

I rolled my eyes as I thought about the new scrumptious

drummer that had just joined our band. *Beyo, was it?* I didn't know his name for sure, but what I did know was that dark and handsome sexy man might just be what I needed to bring some excitement back to my life.

"Oh yeah!" he said as he let go inside of me.

*Shoot, did I take my birth control today?*

He snuggled closer to me. "Woman, that was so good."

I glanced at him and gave a fake smile. Was this the man I fought so hard to have? I was beginning to feel like I had turned into a baby factory and nothing more to him. The passion from our lovemaking was long gone.

"Okay" was my answer.

*I'm going to try one more time before I go and talk to that sexy drummer. Or maybe I could just find another friend. Yeah, I think I might start dating several people like I had originally planned before Khalil came into my life. This monogamy shit is boring me.*

I sat up and pulled my robe on. "Honey, have you thought anymore about my suggestion of us finding a therapist?"

He grunted and turned over. "Amina, I don't have time for that shit right now. I have to work every day to keep a roof over our heads. God knows your gigs at the club won't be paying these bills. If you got a real job, we could have more wiggle room to do some things. Nonetheless, I think we're doing just fine. There's nothing a therapist can tell me about my relationship that I don't already know."

His words cut deep, but that didn't deter me from trying to get my point across one last time. "But, Khalil, I—"

"Let it go! I'm *not* discussing this anymore. You're not going to change my mind."

♬

### Present Day

The banging on my door at 11:00 p.m. startled me. I wasn't expecting anyone at this hour. I fussed, got up, and threw my robe on before I went to the door and peeped out. Khalil's handsome face was the first thing I saw. My eyes widened at the fact that he was standing on my doorstep. He looked pissed and I couldn't say I blamed him.

Thankfully, Adebayo wasn't there.

Because of Khalil's temper, I contemplated what I should do next. There was no doubt he wasn't leaving until he saw me. I slowly unlocked the door and stared into his face without saying a word. For a moment, he didn't speak and held my stare. I finally stepped aside and let him in.

He didn't fully make it inside before he began. "What the hell was all that about tonight? Why were you acting like you lost your mind when you saw me at the restaurant tonight with Sydney?"

He was fuming. He crossed his arms and stared at me. From his stance, I sensed he was not playing with me.

I stared up at him but said nothing as I felt my panties get wet. I hadn't seen him this upset in quite some time. It was sexy to see him taking charge like this. He kept talking and I kept watching the sexy way his mouth moved when he spoke.

"First of all, you don't even know what we were there for."

He was right, I didn't. Still, I didn't like it. "I wasn't aware you two were still in contact," I said.

He sighed and walked over to me. "Should it matter if we are? You've made it quite clear that you don't want to ever get back with me, right?"

I avoided eye contact. I was afraid if he looked into my eyes, he would see what I was trying to cover up. He was wearing me down.

He took a deep breath. "Not that it's any of your business, but Sydney and I bumped into each other a few weeks ago when I went for my doctor's appointment. She said she has some news to share with me, so we exchanged numbers."

I didn't like the sound of that. He had no problems rubbing it in further though.

"Besides, since neither of us are married, I didn't think that would be a problem. I know you think the world revolves around you, but we were friends long before you came into the picture."

"It's not like that, Khalil," I said.

"Really, then what is it like?" he returned.

My silence was my answer. I had no plausible explanation for my behavior.

After a moment, he continued to rub it in. "You can't have it both ways, Amina. Either we're together or not, but I can't continue to play these games with you."

"It's not a game. This is who I am, and you know this."

He crossed his arms again and studied me. "I don't know. Our marriage may have ended because of your boy toy, but any time there's a problem, I'm the first person you call. I see the way you look at me when we're in the same room. I know you still love me. I wouldn't have stayed around this long if I didn't think you did. My question to you would be, what are you *really* running from?"

"He's not my boy toy, and I'm not running from anything. I love him!"

But I was lying. Lying to myself and Khalil. I was running. Running from the pain I feared might happen again if I let Khalil back in. Surely our issues were bound to resurface at some point. Especially since he didn't believe in therapy.

I was also lying about my feelings for Adebayo. I cared for him, and I would even say I had love for him, but I wasn't sure if I was *in* love with him. We bonded through our love of music. And the sex ... it was incredible. I was afraid to lose that. Still, something was missing between the two of us.

Khalil seemed to read my thoughts, and he didn't back down. "Do you really?"

"Yes, I do."

"But you love me more."

I sighed, backed away from him, and made my way to the kitchen. I wasn't going to get pulled into his web.

He wouldn't let me get away that easily though. I felt him on my heels. I spun around to ask him for space, and my body bumped into his.

His body was harder than a man his age had any right to be.

He didn't move. I didn't either. I couldn't.

My bottom bumped the kitchen counter, and I felt his hands begin to roam. He slowly ran the back of his hand down my face, then my collarbone, then my breast. My mouth opened, but I couldn't speak.

He took that as an invitation to insert his tongue into the open space.

He kissed me fervently, and I didn't protest. My head spun with the way he was drinking me in. We kissed like two lovestruck teenagers, and I wondered why he hadn't always touched me this way.

I pulled away long enough to mumble, "Khalil, we can't do this. Bayo and I have a rule—"

"I don't care about your rules … fuck that fool."

This time, he grabbed the back of my head before pressing his lips on mine. In one fell swoop, he lifted me and placed me on the countertop. My head swirled with the amount of passion between the two of us.

He kissed my neck then pulled my shirt up. He bent and slowly placed wet kisses on my stomach. His warm mouth sent shivers up my spine.

Then, he picked me up and carried me out of the kitchen. He headed in the direction of the bedroom but stopped short of entering and put me down in front of the couch.

I figured he was coming to his senses, but I quickly realized he was just getting started. He planted another kiss on my lips, then my neck. He stared into my eyes before grabbing my hand and kissing it. Then he placed it on his crotch.

"See what you're doing to me," he rasped.

I shouldn't have been surprised, but us touching this way felt as if we'd never done it before. It felt new. It almost felt like the first time all over again.

He kissed my lips again before laying me down on the couch. He knelt and lifted my butt slightly as he tugged my pants down. Then, he put his face in my crotch and inhaled my scent.

"Damn, you smell so good, Amina. I can't wait to taste you." He moved my panties to the side. I watched as he bit his bottom lip and touched me down below.

I closed my eyes as his marvelous hands roamed. Then he replaced his hands with his mouth. I gasped when his lips touched my forbidden spot. His hands massaged my nipples as his tongue massaged my clit. There was nothing I could do except cry out for him as an earth-shaking orgasm ran through me.

He was pulling out all the stops. If I wasn't mistaken, it even seemed as if his giving-head skills had improved.

He came up for air and licked his lips. "Damn, woman," he said.

I attempted to get up to return the favor, but he wouldn't let me. "No, baby. Tonight is all about you."

I couldn't remember him saying those words during our marriage, so I stared down at him wide-eyed as he ran kisses up my stomach to my breasts. He put each one in his mouth while playing with the other, then he licked my shoulders and neck.

I moaned.

I reached down and unbuckled his pants. They fell around his ankles. He stepped out of them, then removed his boxer briefs. He leaned down and kissed me slowly. I moaned and stared up at him as he entered me. I closed my eyes as he stretched me to the limit. If I had forgotten how well he was packing, he damn sure reminded me.

He moved his hips slowly at first, but soon moved faster. I matched his thrusts with my own to show him I still had it.

"Oh my God! What are you doing to me?" I cried.

He removed a stray dreadlock from my face and stared into my eyes. He moved his hips in a circular motion and thrust harder. "Baby, you feel so good!" he panted.

"Oh, Khalil!"

"God, Amina!"

I opened my mouth, and my eyes grew wide as another orgasm shot through me. "Awwwww! Shit, baby, it's so good!" I yelled.

My words only caused his hip thrusts to speed up. *Where was this man getting all this energy from?*

He pulled out and picked me up before sitting on the couch. Then he placed me in his lap.

We stared into each other's eyes as I rolled my hips, flexed my pussy muscles, and bucked on his dick. We were like two ravenous animals.

This was the passion he had given me in the very beginning of our marriage. It was the passion I had longed for to show he still loved me even when things got tough. It was unbridled and raw, animalistic but sweet. It was love, and it scared me.

"I love you, baby!" he growled.

"I love you, too!" I cried.

I was sure the neighbors knew our names.

He grunted a few times, then he let go.

I knew I was in trouble.

# Crazy in Love

The next morning, I laid on Khalil's outstretched arm. To say I slept well that night would've been a lie. I would've loved to say the way he put it on me had me sleeping like a baby, but two more rounds of mind-blowing sex and a snoring ex-husband later had my stomach in knots.

*Oh my God! What have I done?*

For the first time in a long while, I felt guilty about my choices. I hated feeling like I betrayed Adebayo. He didn't ask for much, but the one person he had specifically asked me not to be with was lying here in my bed. I wanted to bask in the moment, but knowing that I had opened Pandora's box with Khalil was haunting me.

When I really thought about it though, part of the reason for me having an open relationship *was* so we could see other people. Adebayo knew that. Annoyance sparked in my chest. Was Adebayo trying to control me just as Khalil had before?

I sat up, leaned against the headboard, and stared down at Khalil. I traced the outline of his perfect nose with my finger and smiled when I thought about our last few hours together. I missed being with him like this.

I was plagued with emotions, and my mind and heart raced as I thought about what had happened between us. What was wrong with me? There was no rhyme or reason for why I felt weak every time I was in his presence. Even after all these years, and especially when I already had a great man in my life. I had managed to evade Khalil's advances for this long. What was it about this time? Was it seeing him with his ex that pushed me over the edge? Would this have happened eventually if I hadn't seen them together the night before?

I had promised to never let myself feel intimidated by another woman, but because of their dating history, she was different. Even though he had chosen me, she would always remain my competition when it came to him. I had a lot of nerve though, especially since I was the one who broke their relationship up in the first place.

Still, the night before Khalil had touched me in ways I never thought possible. When we were married, I couldn't recall the last time he'd made love to me like he did that night. He showed the hell out. This man had more stamina than a man his age had any business having.

I was impressed but plagued with uncertainty. Where was

this man when we were married? If I left Adebayo for Khalil, would he go back to his old ways?

He stirred and unexpectedly glanced up at me.

I grabbed my phone and pretended to look for something in it.

He yawned then stretched. "Hey. Up so soon?"

"Your snoring kept me up," I teased.

"Oh ... my bad. The doctor says I need ..." He stopped and scrunched his forehead in thought then snapped his fingers. "One of those machines. He thinks I might have sleep apnea."

"Mm-hmm. I see."

He rubbed his eyes. "You are especially glowing this morning," he added.

My neck grew hot. "Am I?"

He grinned deviously. "Why don't you lie with me a little while longer? I want to feel your body against mine again."

I couldn't make sense of feeling so vulnerable around a man I was once married to for so long. "Unfortunately, I can't. I have a lot to do today. In fact, I can't believe I slept so long," I lied.

"Oh, I see."

"Khalil ... we need to talk about last night," I said. I was afraid of what I was feeling, and I wasn't sure what the next steps should be with us. All I knew was the night before wasn't just going to go away.

"And this morning," he added playfully.

"Yes, that too."

He sat up slowly and leaned on the headboard beside me. "Okay." His demeanor changed. There was no doubt he wouldn't be happy with my next words. But I had to be honest. "Before you say anything, can I say something first?" he said.

I wondered why it couldn't wait, but I didn't object. "Okay. Sure."

"I still love you. I never stopped, but you know that already."

I nodded.

"And your actions last night showed that you still love me too."

"Of course I still love you, Khalil."

We both became silent.

"So, there should be nothing to prevent us from being together then, right?" he asked.

"You know it's not that simple."

"It could be. If you let it be."

"Khalil … I can't." Could I trust him to give me what was missing during our marriage? Would I be a fool to leave a sure thing to be with a possibility?

"And why is that? Because of this *little situation* or so-called *romance* you have going on?"

His horns were showing. The fact that he was reducing my relationship to a "little situation" reminded me how egotistical he could be at times. Adebayo was only half of the equation, and he knew that.

"Don't do that. You know it's more than him. Our relationship wasn't exactly a bed of roses, either."

He wrinkled his brow. "What's that supposed to mean?"

I rubbed my eyes. This conversation was going left … quickly. "It means loving each other was never the issue. You were downright selfish and tried to control me during our marriage. You wouldn't even see a therapist to help save the marriage."

"I wasn't selfish, I—"

"Khalil, please let me finish."

He became silent, which surprised me. That would've never happened when we were married.

The old Amina would have shut down and let him tell me what I should do. But the biggest thing I appreciated about being in my fifties was that now I wouldn't let myself be ma-nipulated. I had complete agency over my body and my life. It felt good. Damn good.

"As I said, you tried to control me when we were married. There was never any doubt you loved me, but you also thought things should always be your way. I don't think you could ever understand who I was."

He frowned and worry lines creased his forehead. "I see."

I adjusted my position on the bed and turned to com-pletely face him. "Do you really? Do you think you could truly love me for who I am now?"

He closed his eyes. "And who is that woman now?"

I took a beat and picked my next words carefully. "I'm a woman who genuinely wants *a partner*. Someone who does not mind listening to me and attending to what I want and need at times. I want someone who won't attempt to quelch me being me and try to mold me into what he wants me to be. I want to be free. Free to live out my desires and passions. I can't live any other way."

He leaned his head on the headboard and spoke lowly. "I didn't realize you saw me that way. I thought I protected you throughout our marriage. I always wanted what was best for you and our girls."

I sighed and touched his forearm. "You did, Khalil. In fact, you *over*protected us. And for that, I'm grateful. But you also brought me back to my childhood when my mother would talk down to me, and that scared me. You treated me like a child. You didn't take my sexual needs seriously. You viewed my music as only a hobby. You never understood it was my *dream*."

I was ecstatic that I could express to him in just a few short moments what I couldn't express to him during our whole marriage.

"I see. Well, the one thing I can tell you is that I'm no longer that person. I'm proud of you and what you've done with your career. You're amazing, and I would never stand in your way again."

I smiled inwardly. It felt good hearing those words from him. "Thank you. That means the world to me, Khalil." I paused as I played with one of my dreadlocks and stared at him. "Do you think you'd be able to adapt to the lifestyle I have now?"

He sighed and gazed into my eyes. The pain of our

complicated situation was etched on his face. "With every-thing inside of me, I want to be with you, and *only* you. I can't promise that I'd ever be okay sharing you. That's not who I am."

His words weren't surprising, but still, I held out hope that he would eventually change his mind. They said love could conquer all, right?

We both grew silent. I still had to know one more thing, though. It was the major downfall of our marriage. It was the bullet I always tried to dodge.

"Are you still in love with her? You never finished telling me what Sydney had to tell you and why you needed to be hanging out again."

He wrinkled his forehead. "What? Wait a minute. Was the reason you showed out last night because you want to be back with me, or because you saw me with Sydney?"

I bit my lip. I didn't know what to say, so I said nothing.

He shook his head. "The kiss. This is about the kiss I shared with her during our marriage, huh? You still can't let it go. After all I just said, that's the only thing you're worried about? Sydney and I hanging out? Are you serious? This is … unfuckinbelievable! I'm here with you, and all you can think about is her!" He threw his hands up.

He was doing what he usually did when things got uncom-fortable: disregarding my feelings. Instead of taking account-ability, he turned it around on me. But that kiss meant more than he could comprehend.

I raised my eyebrows and remained quiet while he continued his rant.

"Maybe we're just too different. We want different things. Maybe this is one of those situations where love just isn't enough."

I panicked and my stomach churned. "What do you mean? Love is always enough!"

Suddenly, he turned his back to me. He reached over and pulled his shirt on before standing up.

I reached for him, but he stepped out of my range.

I hated myself for allowing him to reel me back in. For reminding me what we *could* be, then snatching it away. "Where are you going? We haven't finished talking."

He stepped into his boxers and continued to get dressed. "I should've known. I see what you're doing. You would do anything to keep me away from her, huh?"

I stared at him in disbelief, crossing my arms. How had we gotten here? "Well, now that you mention it, you're right, she's *not* my favorite person. She's complicit for hanging around even after we got married."

He paced the room aggressively. "See, that's what I'm talking about! You've been blaming the wrong person. If you're mad at someone, be mad at *me*. I was the one who took vows, remember? You know how much I cared for her. In fact, I would've married her if you never came into the picture. Honestly, although you're the woman I desired more, I've wondered at times if I made the wrong decision. She would've probably never cheated on me or left me for some punk like this boy toy you left me for."

He always knew how to stomp all over my heart.

I looked away from him and wiped my eyes. As painful as his words were, I needed to hear them. I didn't like it, but it was his truth. It was *our* truth. On several occasions, I wished I had never seen Khalil at the club on that fateful night. Other than my girls, I wondered if our never meeting would have saved me from the pain I felt now that we were apart.

I'd seen this situation time and time again. Two people who were so in love, they had no business being apart—yet there was that one huge thing they just couldn't seem to get past. I'd told my daughter just because you love someone, it didn't mean you were meant to be together. Why couldn't I take my own advice? I wished I could turn my love for him off with the touch of a button like I did with a light switch.

But he wasn't done. I stayed silent as he continued. "The way my relationship ended with her was messed up. Truth be told, if anyone should hate anyone, it should be her hating *us*. I let her go to be with *you*. Because I love *you*! Stop blaming everyone else for flaws in *our* marriage, and *your* failure to commit!"

I opened my mouth to speak but was cut off again.

"Oh, and one more thing. I know he hurt you bad, but I'm *not* Malcolm."

I didn't move as he grabbed his keys and made his way out the door.

# Afraid of Love

"So, let's get to the juicy shit. Let's talk about you and Khalil getting back together. It's about damn time!" Joy exclaimed, clasping her hands, kicking her feet, and stirring the water in the pool. I was sure her boisterous laughter could be heard down the block.

The water from her celebratory kicking splashed, and I shook my head as I used the back of my hand to dry the droplets that made it to my face.

We made small talk at first, but it didn't take her long to want to discuss my drama with Khalil. As usual, my friend had only heard what she wanted to.

I rolled my eyes and put my sunglasses back on. "That's *not* what I said. I *said* we slept together, as in we *fucked*."

She threw her head back and laughed again. "But you haven't slept with him in years. Something happened for you to mess with Khalil again. Admit it, you still want him back, don't you?"

I shook my head but couldn't help but chuckle at her giddiness. She'd been hoping we'd come to our senses for years and get back together. What she failed to realize was that Khalil and I hadn't been able to work out our issues.

"Dang, I'm surely going to miss this place," she said as she closed her eyes and soaked up the sun.

"You don't have to go, you know. Stay with me for a while … at least until you figure things out."

She and her soon-to-be-ex-husband had found a buyer for their family home. It was a condition of the divorce that they sell the home and divide the profits. But, for Joy, looking at another mortgage was something she didn't think made sense with the exorbitant prices for homes in Miami. She had found a somewhat reasonable studio in the Georgia area.

"Thanks, my friend. I appreciate you offering that, but I'm not trying to crowd your space; plus, I think the change will be good. Georgia, here I come!" She laughed.

"Yeah, you and everyone else," I mused. "But, if you change your mind, I'll be here."

She nodded.

My girls and my granddaughter, along with Adebayo and Zion, were coming by my house for a BBQ and I wanted to make sure I caught her up before they arrived. Truthfully, I was surprised I'd managed to keep my night with Khalil from her for this long, but I wanted time to think without any outside influences.

We grew silent.

She turned her attention back on me when she noticed I'd grown distant. "What's up, friend? Talk to me."

My question was simple. "What about Adebayo? I broke his first cardinal rule about not messing with exes."

Again, silence filled the space between us. I closed my eyes and leaned my head back to soak up the sun.

Finally, she spoke. "You're fifty-three years old, Amina. This ain't your first rodeo. Do you *want* to be with Khalil or not?"

"I do, but suppose I can't give him what he wants? Suppose he goes back to his old ways in and out of the bedroom? I mean, Khalil and I already failed at this once. He even went as far as to mention that he wasn't Malcolm, and how he felt I was only pining for him because I saw him with Sydney."

Joy raised her eyebrows. "Whoa, slow down, hon … Malcolm, huh? That's a name I haven't heard in a while."

I frowned when she repeated his name and my thoughts drifted back—way back, to the day after my seventeenth birthday.

When Malcolm came into my life, I thought he was my soulmate. We had so much in common: we were both artists and we wanted to take over the world together. I had caught the bus to meet up with Malcolm at our usual spot. We had decided to run away together to California to pursue our careers (me as a singer and him as an actor), live out the rest of our wild lives together, and give the finger to everyone who didn't think a career in the arts and our undying love could ever sustain us.

An hour passed, and I checked my watch as I waited with bated breath for his arrival. There was no sign of him. Still, I held out hope. After another forty-five minutes and still no sign of him, I went to the pay phone and dialed his number. There was no answer. I slightly panicked when I realized he had never stood me up before, so there must've been something wrong with him.

I dug in my purse for the change that had settled at the bottom, and thankfully I had just enough to get a bus pass to his place. When I got there, I knocked several times but got no answer. My knocks soon turned to banging, then yelling his name before the door finally creaked open. A half-naked woman appeared with a robe on. She struggled to close it slightly as she strained to focus her attention on me. Her hair stood on the top of her head—a testament to what she'd been doing a few minutes before.

Malcolm appeared behind her, his eyes glossy from whatever substance he was consuming. He held a bottle up to his head. "Hey, baby," he said and took a swig.

I glanced between the two of them. "What's going on here?"

He swiped at his nose but didn't say anything.

Tears sprung to my eyes. "I waited almost two hours for you at the bus station. How could you do this to me?"

He stepped outside the house and stared down at me. His

eyes held a hint of regret, and he paused before he spoke. "It was never supposed to happen this way."

I glanced behind him as the woman stepped outside too and put her arm around his waist. "Oh, he didn't tell you?"

I narrowed my eyes at her. "Tell me what?"

She put her hand on her stomach and beamed with pride.

Malcolm focused his gaze on the sidewalk—his way of letting me know he wasn't trying to make eye contact.

"We're pregnant!" she exclaimed.

My heart pounded, and it felt as if I would pass out. I took a few steps backward.

He reached for me, but I turned and fled down the sidewalk. I heard him calling my name, but I never looked back.

"Amina! A ... min ... a."

I opened my eyes and looked over at Joy when I realized she was calling my name.

"Did you hear a word I just said?" she asked.

I shook my head.

"I was just *saying* that you can't compare Khalil to Malcolm. You know that man was on something. If you ask me, I think you're just scared. And from what you told me the other night, Khalil put it on you like when you were first married. It seems like he's grown. If he wasn't ready for you before, he seems like he's ready now. You know how the saying goes: if you love something, let it go, if it's meant ... yadda, yadda, yadda. It sounds like you two might be making your way back to each other."

I kept my eyes closed as I contemplated her statement. She was right. The other night had felt so right. It was almost too good to be true.

But she wasn't done. "I don't know, Amina. Going through my divorce and knowing there is no way in hell I would want to get back with my husband, after all he put me through, it's good to see real love. You have the chance to do it all over again with a man who loves you … a man who's always loved you."

"Adebayo loves me too though. Very much, in fact, and I just don't know if Khalil and I will ever be able to get it together. We're so … different. He can be such an asshole at times."

Honestly speaking, I didn't know what to think after the way Khalil had stormed out of my condo the other night. I couldn't understand why things with us always had to be so difficult. Whoever said love could conquer all, lied. Adebayo was definitely the safer choice, but of course, I didn't like safe. Safe was boring to me. I hadn't made it this far in this world from being safe.

Joy pulled her sunglasses down over her eyes and leaned her head back to join me in enjoying the sun.

"What man isn't," she answered matter-of-factly. "Plus, different can be good. Especially for you. We all know you have a very short attention span when it comes to men."

"Hey, watch it now!"

We both laughed.

"I'm just saying. All I know is you're in quite a precarious situation, my friend. You will ultimately *have* to choose or risk losing them both."

As usual, Joy had given me more to think about than I wanted to. I went to answer when we heard the sliding door open.

Adebayo and Zion had arrived with items for the BBQ. Never one to not notice a good-looking man, Joy leaned over to me. "Is that Zion? He's looking goodt!"

I rolled my eyes and chuckled at my friend. "Joy, stop. You're old enough to be that boy's mother!"

She playfully gasped and put her hand to her chest. "Whatever! I'm old, not dead." She paused. "Wait, fuck that. I'm not old either, and furthermore, I know you're not talking. You're the Head Cougar in Charge. H-C-I-C!"

I threw my head back and laughed at my friend's candor. She was correct. I attracted the young men; everyone knew Adebayo was several years younger than me. In fact, he was seven years my junior. Still, I had my limits. I didn't want to date anyone under forty.

She pulled out a cigarette and repeated herself. "Like I said before, he's looking good, shit!"

I frowned and wrinkled my nose. "Joy, what are you do-ing? Don't you light that mess around me. And when did you start smoking again?"

"Oh yeah. Lately, I have one every now and then. This divorce stuff has me messed up ... don't act like that. I know you puff every now and then too." She put the cigarette to her lips and pulled her lighter out.

I grabbed it before she could light it. "Weed, *not* nicotine. And I don't want you smoking that stuff around my family. I have something you can puff on later though. Something that *won't* kill you."

Her eyes lit up. "Word?"

I chuckled then winked at her. "Word. I'll be back."

I got up and went over to the men. I gave Adebayo a quick kiss and hugged Zion.

My king was looking good. Really good. I knew I would have to tell him about Khalil sooner than later, so I leaned up and whispered in his ear before I lost my nerve, "Remind me to tell you something later."

"Everything okay?" he asked.

"Sure," I lied.

He nodded and held up the bags. "Okay. Let me get this stuff on the grill." He went to the kitchen with Zion in tow.

Not too long after, my daughters arrived, and the party really got started.

Seeing my children, but especially my grandchildren, made me forget about the stress I had caused myself regarding my lover and ex-husband.

We laughed, ate, and reminisced over the next few hours.

When everyone had left and the house was silent, I questioned if telling Adebayo about my and Khalil's sexcapades even made sense, but I couldn't with good conscience pretend that nothing happened.

We cleaned up and got ready for bed. Adebayo came over to me and put his arms around me. As usual, he wanted to play before we slept. "My queen, today was amazing."

He leaned down and kissed me. Normally, his kiss would have lit a fire in me, but I had to admit, I was lukewarm. I closed my eyes and pulled his face down for a deeper kiss. I hoped kissing him could erase the other night with Khalil from my mind.

This time he pulled back. He studied me. Years of being together made it hard not to be transparent. He furrowed his brow. "You alright?" he asked.

I smiled at him awkwardly. Kissing him didn't feel right after the rendezvous with my ex-husband. "Of course, I am," I lied. "Why do you ask?"

"Something just seems … off with you. I can't put my finger on it." I pulled away from him, and he followed me. "Does this have to do with whatever it was you wanted to tell me earlier?"

He was reading me. I felt like a nasty book, but the moment of reckoning was here.

I grabbed his hands, sat, and pulled him down on the bed. He stared at me as he waited for me to divulge whatever was making me distant.

"So … yes, this has everything to do with what I mentioned earlier."

He furrowed his brows. "Okay ... so, what's going on?"

"I slept with someone."

He let go of my hands and raised his eyebrows. He nodded. "Oh." Although it may have thrown him for a loop, I knew he wouldn't be upset because of the nature of our relationship. "I'm surprised we didn't speak about it beforehand like we normally do. In fact, I haven't even heard you say you were interested in anyone lately."

I shifted uncomfortably. "Yeah, it was *kind of* unexpected." Again, I knew I wasn't saying anything out of the ordinary for us.

He crossed his arms and studied me. "Oh. Okay. Well, where did you meet this person?"

"It's ... umm ... someone I've known for a while."

He narrowed his eyes at me. Obviously, he didn't like where this conversation was going. "Okay."

I squeezed my eyes shut and took a deep breath before I blurted out the next words. "It's Khalil. I slept with Khalil."

When he didn't answer, I slowly opened my eyes.

He sat stoically. I didn't know what to do or say next.

Finally, he spoke. "I guess I shouldn't be surprised. It was only a matter of time. The way you two look at each other when you're in the same room, the fact that you call him for important matters first, instead of your partner ..."

"Bayo, that's not true. I—"

His stare shut me down from conjuring up a comeback. It was cold. I'd never seen him look at me this way. I didn't like it.

"You just couldn't help yourself, huh?"

"I ... I ... it wasn't planned. It just ... happened."

He shook his head in disappointment. I was losing him. I could feel it. "I suppose you're going to tell me you're going back to him too."

I shook my head. "I love you."

"But you love him too."

I wanted to deny my feelings, but I also didn't want to lie anymore. I lowered my eyes before I spoke again. My answer was simple. "Yes, but this is where I want to be. That part of my life is the past. You're my future."

I didn't bother to tell him about Khalil's and my blowup after our sexcapade being the main reason I was still there.

I reached for him.

He moved away from me and stood up. "I'll sleep on the couch tonight, then I'll figure out what to do tomorrow."

I nodded.

He began to make his way out of the room, but before he went out, he stopped, turned around, and smirked. "Oh, and one more thing. I already knew when I saw his car in the driveway overnight. I was just waiting to see how long it would take you to tell me."

My eyes widened. As usual, I was messing up in love.

# Love Less

Adebayo held fast to his promise.

The next morning when I felt his side of the bed, it was cold. There was no denying he was serious because even when we'd had disagreements in the past, he wouldn't have left my side. He surprised me when he lightly tapped on the door and stuck his head in.

I perked up when I saw his face. I smiled and sat up. "Come in! You know you didn't have to knock."

It felt as though I was talking to a stranger.

He cautiously entered the room, crossed his arms behind him, and leaned against the wall. He appeared so innocent. He appeared wounded. He appeared lost.

I hated that I was the cause of his pain.

"So, I'm getting ready to go back to my place, and wanted you to know," he said.

I nodded but didn't want to give up that easily. "Can I call you later?"

He reluctantly shook his head. "I need some time to think."

I wanted to respect his wishes but knew too much time to think would give him an out. Every time I'd heard that in the past, it never worked in my favor.

I got up and strode over to him, and he stood up straight as an arrow.

I slowly touched his face. "I hate that I broke your trust, and I'm truly sorry, but I love you, Bayo."

He nodded. "I know you do, but is it enough? Will I ever be enough for you? Will you be able to stay away from *him*?"

I removed my hand and stepped back. I didn't want to make any promises I couldn't keep. "We only have today. Let's concentrate on the here and now."

He smirked. "Yep, that's about right. I figured you'd say something like that. Excuse me." He stepped around me and left.

Two days later, I was surprised when my phone rang and his name flashed across the screen. I answered apprehensively. Fear of him announcing the end of our relationship consumed me.

To my surprise, he sounded pleasant, almost too excited to speak. He suggested we meet at a local coffee shop to talk. That was more than I expected, so I was more than happy to oblige.

When I saw Adebayo, he was freshly shaven. Something I'd noticed he'd eased up on lately. I went over to him and we embraced. It felt good being in his arms again. He pulled out my chair. "Shall we?"

I eyed him suspiciously. He was way too calm after the other night.

We ordered our drinks and sipped on them for a while. Tension filled the space between us.

Finally, he broke the silence. "Is that a new nose ring? I really like that on you."

I appreciated that he noticed everything about me. I blushed. "Why, thank you. Yes, it is."

"Of course. So, my queen. I want to ask you something."

I nodded and took a sip of my latte. "Okay. What would that be?"

He cleared his throat and leaned into the space between us. "What if we clean the slate and start over?"

I blinked a few times and furrowed my brow. "What do you mean?"

He smiled at me. There was no doubt he'd thought this through. "What if we have one last tryst? Take a swinger's cruise, meet up with other couples, have some fun, and get this out of our system."

"Get this out of *our* system?" I repeated.

"Yes, *this* lifestyle. I've reached the end of my rope. As I've said in the past, I'm tired. I want a *normal* relationship."

I'd seen this moment coming at some point, but not this

soon. There was no doubt that my being with Khalil had expedited the process. "Okay. I like the idea of a cruise. I think it would be great to get away given that our relationship has been strained lately, and … well … of course, what happened with Khalil the other night. But …"

"But, what?"

"Well, what if I'm not on the same page after the cruise? What if I'm not ready to give you monogamy or marriage?"

He sat back in his chair and narrowed his eyes at me. He shrugged. "Well, I'll be done."

I was pretty sure I wasn't ready to let him go in that moment; unfortunately, I felt backed into a corner since I was already on thin ice with him. I didn't want to let him go without giving this thing one last try. I owed that to him and myself.

"Okay, let's do this," I said apprehensively.

I held on to the hope that we would have such a good time, he would change his mind.

# Birthday Love

I spent the next few weeks throwing myself into my music, planning my middle daughter's thirtieth birthday party, and taking time to myself. As I planned the party, I thought about Adebayo's and my upcoming cruise and dreaded the inevitable outcome. There was no doubt our lives were going to change one way or another when we got off our trip, and I highly doubted he would change his mind about wanting to settle into a marriage. I selfishly dreaded losing him as my comfort blanket.

Before I knew it, the day of Anisa's party had arrived. Everything was coming together beautifully. I was glad I had the chance to do this party for her, being that she was turning the big three-zero. She wasn't feeling good about where she was in her life, so hopefully we could make a moment that would remind her how amazing she was. Also, she had finally agreed to perform a song with me! It had been ages since I'd been able to be on the stage with her, so nothing gave me more joy than having her showcase her God-given talent on such a special occasion.

I was also glad I could see the three of my daughters at the same time. Everyone was so busy these days, it was hard for us to get together as a family.

What I was most anxious about, though, was having the two men I cared about in the same room at the same time, especially after what had gone down with Khalil. My anxiety didn't lie either. The tension between us could be cut with a knife. Every so often, I would catch the two of them exchanging glares, but they managed to stay out of each other's way. Thankfully, being busy with our daughters also gave Khalil little time to act up.

It was the story of our lives. Khalil would never like Adebayo, and Adebayo would always be insecure about my relationship with Khalil. It was a no-win situation for all of us. Whatever it may be, though, I didn't care how much discord the three of us had; nothing was going to ruin this moment for my daughter. At least, that's what I hoped.

The band and I had gone over the songs we were dedicating to my daughter, and I had even written one for her. The moment I was most excited about was when she and I would sing together. It was something I lived for since I hadn't been able to get my daughter on stage since she was a teenager because of her struggles with her self-esteem. I had taken a shot in the dark by asking her if she would mind performing a song or two with her old girl, and surprisingly she agreed. Actually, I was flabbergasted at her response. So she wouldn't have a chance to change her mind, I wasted no time finding songs for us to perform and sending them over to her.

After the band did their thing, we continued to enjoy the festivities as several poets recited their poetry in her honor. One of the poets pulled up a chair onstage and had Anisa sit there while he serenaded her with his words. She blushed when he grabbed her hand and kissed it.

Soon afterward was the moment I had been waiting for all night. The moment Anisa and I had spent hours rehearsing for. It was also a moment I knew we would never forget. I got up and made my way to the stage, then I invited Anisa to join me. I could tell how nervous she was as she got up and wiped her hands on her dress, nervously looking around the room. I smiled at her because I was familiar with that feeling and had learned how to breathe through the nerves. She may have been nervous now, but I knew she would thank me later. I gave my cue for the band to start playing and sang like my life depended on it, then I gave her the signal to come in.

I heard the nerves in her voice with her first notes, but I had faith in her.

*Breathe and find your center, baby girl. Just like I taught you.*

And that's what she did. As expected, my daughter over delivered. She closed her eyes, let loose, and hit every note perfectly. Then she opened her eyes and sang louder. I watched as the audience moved to the music. There was something in her gaze when she was singing, and tears sprang to my eyes. I got it. It happened every time I performed as well. It was that euphoric feeling a person got when they were living their purpose. If that wasn't enough confirmation, when we finished the song, the audience stood up and applauded loudly.

Anisa and I grinned at each other and embraced. I was happy we could share this moment together.

I wiped my tears and said, "Anisa, that was absolutely amazing!"

She wiped her tears as well. "Thank you, Iya. For everything."

I nodded but spotted my mother and sister in the crowd. "I'll be right back, queen," I said before making my way over to greet them.

I said a prayer. Hopefully, they wouldn't ruin the good vibes I was feeling.

"Hey, Jackie! Hello, Mom!" I said when I reached them.

Jackie got up to give me a hug but, as usual, my mother's face was stone cold. I ignored her attitude, bent, and hugged her as if I didn't detect she was not happy with something.

"Are you having a good time? Did you ladies enjoy the songs?" I asked.

Jackie jumped up and snapped her fingers excitedly. "Sis, I may not care for your lifestyle, but I can *never* talk shit about your voice. As usual, y'all were amazing!"

I beamed with pride, but as with any time I was around my mother, my happiness didn't last long.

My mother frowned at her. "Jackie, watch your mouth!" she fussed.

Jackie pouted. "Well, they were *really good*, Mom. I couldn't help myself. Sorry, I got a little carried away."

I narrowed my eyes at her and shook my head. Was my grown-ass sister *really* apologizing about a little curse word? In that moment, I was reminded of why I was thankful that I had managed to move out of Mom's vice grip at seventeen and forge a life for myself. She still had a strong hold on Jackie.

My mother cleared her throat but didn't make eye contact. "It was okay. Your voice cracked a little on that high note though."

I rolled my eyes.

I didn't want to toot my own horn, but I knew we had given a damn good performance. No matter what I did, this woman would never be happy with me. She would always find something wrong.

Again, I ignored my mother's bad behavior and tried to make light of the situation. "Maybe I'll let you give me voice lessons again, Mom. No one does it better than you."

For a moment, she focused her attention on me. I thought I caught a glimpse of rare happiness in her eyes. Unfortunately, we were interrupted when Jackie looked around me and squinted toward the stage.

"What the … ?"

I turned around just in time to see who I *thought* was Anisa's *ex*-boyfriend, Terrence, hand her a bouquet of flowers.

"She's been awesome to me," he said, "and I wanted to let you all know how much I appreciate her." He was putting on a good show, but I saw right through him. His words felt robotic … almost rehearsed. There was no passion in what he was putting down.

The crowd grew silent when he grabbed the microphone. "And one more thing." We watched as he went back over to my daughter and lowered himself to one knee.

My mouth dropped in horror when I realized what he was about to do.

"Anisa, will you marry me?"

I shook my head and prayed her common sense would take over. But common sense and love didn't usually live in the same space. I knew that well enough.

"Yes, Terrence. I'll marry you!" she cried.

I dropped my head into my hands because I felt sick to my stomach. I sucked it up quickly though, and made up my mind to support my daughter in the best way possible. She would need it in the long run, because there was no way this man was right for her.

I wasn't the only one who obviously had issues with what was going on. I heard my other daughter, Talia, as well as Anisa's friend, Monique, share some not-so-nice choice words.

If I thought that wasn't enough, Khalil clearly wanted to hurt the young man and began to stomp across the room. Thankfully, Talia's husband and Adebayo were there to step in.

My mother leaned over to Jackie and asked, "Didn't she

just break up with her boyfriend? Who is this guy? Please tell me it's not the same loser."

She had gotten it right this time. For the first time in a while, I couldn't disagree with her.

As Adebayo and I slept the next morning, I was awakened by Khalil's call. Adebayo looked up, no doubt annoyed, but didn't say anything. He turned onto his stomach and attempted to go back to sleep.

I sat up and hit the answer button. Khalil didn't wait for me to speak.

"What the hell is going on with our daughter?"

"What do you mean?"

I yawned a few times and rubbed my eyes as Khalil ranted. Was he serious? Couldn't this have waited? Most would argue that our daughters were grown and should have been making their own decisions regarding their lives, but as I'd said before, I wasn't traditional. *We* weren't traditional. Khalil and I had vowed to always be there for our daughters as a unit no matter how old they got. Still, I would've appreciated a few more hours of sleep after Anisa's party because I was worn out. Not to mention, I probably wouldn't hear the end of this from Adebayo.

"One minute she's crying about this man hurting her and whatnot, then the next minute she's accepting a proposal. That young man hasn't made any attempts to reach out to me to talk about marrying our daughter after that debacle at her house the other day, or last night. Did he reach out to you?"

"No, he didn't." It would've been a nice gesture for Terrence to ask us for Anisa's hand in marriage, but honestly, that was the least of my problems with him. This was a different generation, so I wasn't trippin' off that. But, from everything Anisa had told me about Terrence in the past, he was a liar and a cheater who treated her like shit.

"I wanted to hurt him last night after that proposal shit he pulled at her party."

"I could tell."

"Well, I need to talk to Anisa about this. We *all* need to talk to her."

I rolled my eyes. Did Khalil even sleep last night? He couldn't have.

"I hear you, but you do realize this isn't our decision, right?"

"It may not ultimately be my decision, but she's going to hear what I have to say. My daughter can do much better than this Terrence guy."

I closed my eyes and pinched the bridge of my nose. I agreed with Khalil. My daughter could do a hell of a lot better. I knew my ex-husband wouldn't let this go, so I got up and walked out of the bedroom. "What do you suggest we do, Khalil?"

"I already called and told her I'll be over later. Around six. Will you be available then?"

"Well actually, Adebayo and I—"

"Oh, he can wait. I'll pick you up around 5:45."

I wanted to tell him hell no, and that he needed to go back to bed, but I quickly realized it would probably be better if I was there to help referee the situation.

I sighed. "Okay, I guess."

"Cool. I'll see you then." He disconnected the call before I had a chance to protest.

When I turned to go back to the room, Adebayo was leaning against the doorframe.

I didn't have to say anything for him to know what was going on. "Let me guess. Family issues, and I'm not invited," he said.

I opened my mouth to speak, but before I could say anything, he turned around, went back into the bedroom, and shut the door behind him.

# Frustrated by Love

had a feeling Anisa wouldn't be pleased with all of us ambushing her and showing up unexpectedly at her home, but I decided to go along with Khalil's plan anyway.

By all indications, my instincts were correct, because when she opened the door and saw me, her sisters, and Khalil standing there, she made a face and rolled her eyes before reluctantly moving aside and allowing us to enter. Her best friends Monique and Jamie were also at her home to add their two cents.

We got seated and took turns expressing our dislikes about her relationship with her now-fiancé. We wanted her to see why we didn't think he was good for her, but it was Khalil and Talia who were doing the most.

Khalil: "I want to know what's really going on with this man."

Nia: "Are you sure Terrence is what you want? I mean, look at my life."

Talia: "What were you thinking?"

Me: "Are you sure this is really what you want, and who you want it with?"

Anisa: "We've been talking, and we realized that we want to be together."

Monique: "What about his baby mama?"

Talia: "Yeah, that."

Anisa: "He let me know they're no longer together."

Talia: "And you believed him?"

Monique: "So, he wants you now, being that she no longer wants his ass."

Anisa: "No. He wants me because he loves me and sees that I'm the better woman for him."

There was a collective sigh in the room.

Talia shook her head and covered her face with her hand. "Oh my God, how ignorant can you really be?"

Me: "Talia, that's not helping."

Khalil: "All I know is that if this Terrence guy hurts you again, I can't be held responsible for my actions."

Me: "Khalil, you know that's not the answer."

Khalil: "It's my answer."

Anisa seemed flustered as we went back and forth. I could tell she was about to blow. However, I didn't realize how far she would go until she blurted …

"Iya hasn't been perfect in her relationships, and while

everyone is going in on my relationship with Terrence, how come no one has mentioned that Nia is having an affair?"

I gasped and my eyebrows rose at her words. It wasn't like my daughter to take her anger out on anyone, and her feeling cornered was no reason for her to act this way. We'd pushed her too far, but still, I was disappointed in her. I didn't care so much that she had spoken about me, but I hated that she had included Nia.

I was also surprised she knew that information about her sister. It didn't take us long to figure out how she knew, though.

Talia balled up her fists as she fussed. "Damn, Anisa. I can't believe you! I told you that in confidence!"

"Oh my goodness. I'm so sorry, Lia," Anisa said.

It was too late though. The damage was already done.

Talia put her hand up. "I'm good!" she fumed. She got up, grabbed her purse, and made her way to the door. "I'm done with this!" she yelled over her shoulder. "I'll be in the car when y'all are ready because I'm tired of trying to save somebody that doesn't want to be saved." With that, she walked out and slammed the door behind her.

Nia had tears in her eyes. Clearly, Anisa's words had also triggered her. "Well, since everyone knows about my affair, I might as well let you all know that my man's name is Devon, and I had a miscarriage as well." She got up and stormed out behind Talia.

Nia and Anisa's relationship was strained, so I was surprised she would continue to chime in. There was no doubt she was upset that Anisa brought up her affair. I also felt horrible about the timing of revealing Nia's miscarriage.

Anisa *did* have a point about calling out Nia and her husband's situation though. Nia's relationship with her husband *was* raggedy. He was a liar and cheater too, so I had no doubt their relationship would be ending at some point soon.

Khalil closed his eyes, leaned forward, clasped his hands together, and rested his chin on his hands. He didn't speak for a few tense moments, and I was afraid of what he would say when he did. When he opened his eyes, disappointment was written all over his face.

He stood up slowly and took a deep breath before speaking his piece. "For the most part, you've been a daughter that's always made good decisions for her life, but for some reason, you keep dropping the ball on your love life. For the life of me, I can't understand it."

"Daddy—" Anisa said.

"Let me finish. I'm going to say this, and then I'm done. Before you go down the aisle with this man, I suggest you take some time out and make sure you know without a shadow of a doubt that it's you he really wants, because we men don't change overnight."

He kissed her forehead and made his way out the door.

Anisa stared at me, and I imagined she wanted me to give my support as I usually did. But I couldn't this time. I had to let her know her behavior was not okay. Especially when we were looking out for her best interests.

I said, "I'm disappointed in you. I knew about your sister's infidelity, but that wasn't your business to tell. Everyone here took the time out today because we all love you and want the best for you. I can understand you feeling the way you feel about what I've done to our family, but I wish you wouldn't have put your sister's business out on front street. She's dealing with enough from her miscarriage, and this was not the time for that. Plus, this moment is about you."

Her tears didn't deter me. I spoke with my hands to let her know I wasn't playing. "You need to take a good look at the discord you're allowing this man to cause in your life, even without him being present today. I was hoping to gain a son, but it feels like I'm losing a daughter. I hope you figure out what demons are causing you to make these poor decisions before you do something you'll live to regret and lose everyone that means something to you." I held on tight for several agonizing moments before I left.

We got in the car, and Khalil angrily reversed out the driveway. He sped down the road, and I feared for my family's lives.

"I can drive if you'd like," I offered.

"I'm good," he answered without so much as a glance in my direction. He wore his heart on his sleeve, so I wasn't surprised at his reaction. The muscle in his jaw was pulsing, a clear indication of how he felt about the outcome of our intervention.

"Well, that was a complete and utter waste of time," Talia said as she rolled her eyes and rubbed her pregnant belly.

I glanced back at her and her sister.

"Yep, in one ear and out the other," Nia added.

"How dare she turn this around on us? Bringing Mom's indiscretions into her mess and bringing in Nia's affair. That was low," Talia said.

I tried to be the peacemaker and redirect the conversation. "Well, to play devil's advocate, her guard was up. She felt ganged up on. I know all about that. Your grandmother and Aunt Jackie used to gang up on me all the time. Believe me when I say it's *not* a good feeling."

"Stop taking up for her, Iya. You always do that," Talia fussed.

"I'm not taking up for her. I'm just saying we all need grace at some point in our lives. When your father cheated on me with his ex …" I stopped abruptly, realizing I had just let the cat out of the bag.

Khalil didn't speak. He kept looking straight ahead as he drove.

Both girls became silent.

"What do you mean when Dad cheated?" Nia asked.

I looked back at the two of them, and Nia looked so innocent. I realized Nia and Talia were much more like me in relationships than I had thought. In fact, all my girls had dealt with or were dealing with infidelity in some form or another. Anisa was just the one whose relationship struggles were out in the open. Not only did she inherit my vocal ability, but she seemed lost, kind of like me.

In all actuality, Talia shouldn't have been judging either. I planned to take what I knew about her marriage to my grave.

And Nia, although she was at the brink of her marriage ending … I could see that the new man in her life might have his own skeletons. I wouldn't tell her that though, because she seemed happy. At least for now.

The girls had always thought I was the sole reason for my and their father's marriage ending, and we never thought to fix what we viewed as unbroken. Although our daughters were grown, I didn't want them to find that information out like this.

I lowered my eyes. "I just meant she didn't always have the best example of what a healthy relationship is supposed to look like."

Khalil finally glanced at me. His jaw was clenched, but he remained silent.

"Well, that's not what you said. You said *when* Dad cheated," Talia pressed.

"You were the one that cheated, right Mom?" Nia asked.

They knew their father wasn't perfect, but when it came to being a faithful husband, he was their role model.

"Without saying much else, I will say we both had indiscretions," Khalil finally chimed in.

I glanced back in time to see my daughters exchange

perplexing glances, and I felt as if I'd just ruined Christmas by telling my children Santa Claus was not real. In just a second, I'd snatched away their fairy tale image of their father.

"Well, she's old enough to know better. I'm *done* trying to change her mind about this fool. If she wants to ruin her life, let her go right on ahead," Talia replied.

"I know that's right. I'm glad we all went to see her and at least let her know our thoughts. She can't ever say we didn't care," Nia added.

I looked back at Nia and shook my head.

Khalil dropped the girls off at their respective homes and the two of us rode together in silence for a while.

Tension was in the air. It wasn't our usual playful, sexual tension either. I couldn't put my finger on it, but there was something different about our interaction.

In a meager attempt to break the ice, I said, "What's going on with us? It feels like you're pulling away since the last time we … you know. Even when we've argued in the past, we would always be able to talk afterward. You seem different."

He shrugged and barely glanced in my direction. "I'm okay. Just adjusting to my new normal."

I narrowed my eyes at him. I wasn't sure I liked where he was going. "Yes, I see you've been scarce lately. We don't have to become strangers, you know."

"I came out last night for Anisa's party and I'm here now, aren't I?"

"You're acting like you don't like me."

He sighed. "That's the problem. I *love* you. Maybe a little too much."

"You know what I mean."

He pulled off the road, stopped in a parking lot, and turned off the engine. He took a deep breath and stared over at me.

I stared back.

"Are you serious? You *know* I could never hate you. You're the only woman who has been able to invigorate and drive me nuts at the same time."

We shared a laugh, and my insides became warm.

He leaned over and put his lips on mine. He kissed me with so much passion, I almost told him we should go ahead and go to the justice of the peace. *Almost.*

He pulled away suddenly. "But you're like poison to my soul. You're the sugar that I enjoy but know I shouldn't have because you're not good for me. That's why I have to let you go."

I frowned. Those weren't the words I hoped to hear. I thought he'd just had a moment the other night when he said that love might not be enough. But now I could see why he was pulling away. My stomach churned with jealousy.

"I need a break from all of this."

"All of what? Our family?"

He shook his head. "Don't do that. I knew you would. You know I'm *always* going to be here for our girls. I just don't think I can be here for … you … at least not in the same way as before. We can't continue to lean on each other like this."

"Khalil, you're one of my best friends." It was Sydney. It

had to be. He'd spent years wanting to get back with me, but now that Sydney was back in the picture, he was waving the white flag on our relationship.

He looked exhausted. He took a deep breath and ran his hands down his face. I didn't know if his exhaustion was from me or the intervention.

"And you're one of mine, but where do we draw the line? How are we supposed to move on with healthy relationships if we stay in each other's lives? Maybe I shouldn't have called you today. I should've just gone by myself to see Anisa, or with Talia and Nia."

I sighed in exasperation. "Of course you should've called."

"I don't know. I can bet what's-his-name wasn't pleased, right?"

I was taken aback by his insight, but I shouldn't have been. Sometimes it felt as if this man knew me better than I knew myself. I wanted to lie and tell him differently, but I couldn't. I shook my head.

"Exactly, and now that I'm going back into the dating pool again, I need to make sure I don't anger whomever I date with our little ... situationship."

My eyes widened at his admission and the fact he had reduced our relationship to a situationship. At least I knew I was correct in my assumptions about another woman. It wasn't fair for me to be jealous, but I was.

He started the car and pulled back onto the road. More tense moments followed in the few remaining blocks to my home. Within minutes, he pulled into my driveway, then leaned over and kissed my cheek. He smiled at me, but his eyes were serious. "Bye, Amina."

I nodded and choked back tears before I got out and shut the car door. Then I watched as he backed out of my driveway, and presumably out of my life.

# Love is Painful

"That's my baby!" My sister yelled as my nephew Kareem made his way across the stage for his long-awaited graduation ceremony. She jumped up and down while wildly clapping her hands.

Kareem's father, Roy, and his new wife sat behind us. We all joined in, screaming at the top of our lungs to show our support. I couldn't have been prouder. I had the same love for my nephew as if he was a child that I bore.

I was dressed in African attire from head to toe as an honor to the ancestors for getting my nephew to this point. My mother sat on Jackie's left side, and I sat on the right. Jackie was the buffer between the two of us. I wasn't sure if my mother and I said more than five words to each other so far that day. After all this time, I couldn't understand how a mother could detest their child as much as she did me.

Sure, when I was younger I didn't follow her rules to a T,

still I never disrespected her while I was in her home. She'd made it quite clear in the past that her issue with me was that I chose to sing in the club instead of for Jesus. Her disapproval was further exacerbated by the fact that I chose to have non-conventional relationships.

It should have been enough that my career had finally taken off. But no matter how hard I tried, nothing I did would ever be good enough for her. I glanced over at her as she smiled from ear to ear and rolled my eyes. I'd never seen her that elated about anything I did. I couldn't even remember her attending my graduation ceremony or coming out to support one of my shows.

I yearned for a healthy mother-and-daughter relationship. My mother could blow, and I even hoped she and I could sing together like Anisa and I used to do when Anisa was younger. However, I realized early on that would probably remain a dream. I had wanted a closer relationship with her when I was young and had even offered to sing at her church from time to time. She wouldn't hear of it though. She would say, "You can't have one foot in with God and the other in the world."

That's why I didn't go to church now. I had decided I would take my talents to where they would be appreciated.

After the commencement activities were done, we stood outside to take pictures with the only reason we were in the same space: my nephew.

When he saw me, his face lit up. I was his favorite aunt, according to him. Hell, I was his only aunt.

"Hey, Auntie Amina!" he said and strode over to me. He posed, popped his collar, and threw up peace signs as I snapped a few pictures of him with my phone.

"So, you made it through undergrad in one piece, huh?" I teased. I had no doubt in my mind that he would've made it with flying colors.

"And you know this! Medical school, here I come!" he boasted.

We laughed some more and left to go to the restaurant where the graduation celebration would continue. Jackie had gotten us a private room in the back. We each went around the table, gifting Kareem or making a speech as a tribute. If I thought the good times would continue rolling, I was sadly mistaken when I handed my nephew his graduation gift.

I'd thought long and hard about what to get him because I wanted to make sure it would be something useful. And what could be more useful than money, especially when it came to college expenses?

I stood and cleared my throat. "My nephew, you are one of the most wonderful humans I have ever known. I know you'll be nothing short of amazing on your next journey, and you can operate on me any time!" I handed him an envelope.

He cheesed, and the room grew silent as everyone watched him remove the check. His eyes got wide when he saw the amount. "Wow … Auntie A, five thousand dollars!"

I beamed with pride that I was blessed to be able to do that for him, but my joy didn't last long.

"Five thousand dollars? Are you out of your mind?" Jackie exclaimed.

My mother nodded in agreement. "Amina, why in the world would you think giving him that much money would be okay?"

I couldn't understand why Jackie was so upset when she had just expressed to me weeks before that she couldn't afford to give him what she felt he deserved.

His father jumped in, probably to keep them from ripping my head off. "I think it's awesome! Jackie, he's a college student, for God's sake. God knows you won't ever be able to do that for him."

Well, at least he started off good … I wish he would've left that last part off.

"I've been the one responsible for most of his care all this time. You think I can't take care of my own son? We could *never* accept that money!" Jackie fussed.

My mom took that as her cue to find something else wrong with me. She glared at me as she spoke. "As always, she's trying to show you up, just throwing that money in your face."

I had no clue what they were talking about. The money was given out of the goodness of my heart. Everyone who knew me knew I would do anything for my nephew. I shook my head in disappointment. "I'm sorry you feel that way."

Jackie spoke again. "We don't need your handouts." She turned to Kareem. "Give your auntie her money back."

"But Mom, I—"

My mom jumped in. "Do as your mother says, Karie."

His father spoke up again. "He's twenty-one now. He doesn't have to do what you say."

My nephew got up and made his way over to me. "Thanks, Auntie A, but it's okay."

I stared at him with my arms folded. "You know you don't have to give it back. You're old enough to make your own decisions."

He smiled. "I know. It's all good, Auntie, but I'll be okay." He handed me the check. "Thanks though."

I shook my head and reluctantly took the check back. I hated to have put my nephew in that position and silently kicked myself for not getting his bank information and putting the money in his account myself. That was one of the reasons I liked to keep things simple. Grandiosity never worked well for me.

His father spoke one final time. "That's messed up, Jackie. As usual, you found a way to make his moment about you."

"Go to hell, Roy," she threw back.

"Dang, y'all. Can't we just enjoy this dinner without arguing this *one* time?" Kareem fussed. He clenched his fists in frustration as our family always had some kind of drama whenever we got together.

He marched out of the restaurant.

Roy threw his napkin down, got up, and followed his son.

I hoped Kareem's being upset would have calmed my mom

down, but it didn't. "Now look what you've done, Amina. Why would you think giving him all that money without running it past us would be okay?"

*Us? Did she just say 'us'?*

As usual, she was giving her unwanted opinion. Somehow, she failed to realize Kareem was Jackie and Roy's son. Not hers.

I rolled my eyes and put a spoonful of veggies in my mouth.

"No answer. I'm not surprised. And another thing. Why haven't I, the woman who birthed you, seen or heard from you since Anisa's birthday party over a month ago?"

There it was. It was no surprise I'd become the topic of discussion.

Slowly, I felt myself unraveling. Add this to how it felt as if my love life was falling apart one piece at a time. I was over it. I was over *her*. If she wanted a fight, she could get one.

I put my fork down and glared at her. "For the same reason I haven't seen or heard from *you*! The phone goes both ways, you know."

She had the nerve to gasp. "You know I won't be here forever. One day you're going to regret the way you treated me. If you weren't out here whoring with God knows who, maybe you could find the time. I guess I can't be mad though. You sleep with so many men, those spirits are probably controlling you. I don't know how that Adebayo guy puts up with your shenanigans."

"Mom!" Jackie gasped.

Jackie's jumping in surprised me. Maybe she realized this

conversation was about to get uglier. Or maybe she wanted to save her ass from being embarrassed since we were in a public setting.

I was hurt that my mother believed I was just some two-dollar whore in the streets. If she took the time to talk to me, maybe she'd understand who I really was.

"Well, I prefer being a *whore* than a tired old bitter bitch. Maybe if you'd live a little, you wouldn't always be so worried about what I'm doing!" I retorted.

Again, gasps could be heard around the table.

"Amina!" Jackie exclaimed.

That didn't stop Mom though. A blind man could see she'd been waiting for this moment. She looked me up and down and spoke while swinging her hands wildly. "You spend all your time dressing up in all your African crap, pretending to be Zen and all that mess. But we know that's to cover up who you really are inside."

I took a deep breath and attempted to tune her out. I wasn't about to keep going back and forth with her. No matter what she said to me, she was still my mother. I had already gone too far.

That was until she said, "You're just like your daddy. No wonder your girls are lost and can't have healthy relationships either!"

"Mom! Stop it!" Jackie yelled. This time she reached over and grabbed Mom's forearm to calm her down.

Hearing her speak about my daddy when he wasn't here

to defend himself brought tears to my eyes, but I wouldn't give her the satisfaction of seeing me cry. She could bash me all she wanted, but talking about my children was off limits. It was the final straw. She no longer had to worry about us because if I had my say, she wouldn't be seeing any of us again.

I removed two hundred-dollar bills from my wallet, threw them on the table, grabbed my things, and dismissed myself from the table without looking back.

# 13

# Intoxicated by Love

I honestly didn't remember how I'd made it home. Thankfully, the Universe had granted me this solid and let me make it in one piece. When I got to my door, I could barely find the opening to insert my key. I took several deep breaths to calm my shaking hands and sent Joy a text to let her know that the night was a hot mess and I would fill her in later. I was overwhelmed by what had just happened at the graduation dinner. How could a celebratory event turn so sour? Instead of celebrating my nephew, we managed to make the event all about our dysfunctional relationship. Usually, I didn't hang on to anger this long, but my mother always had a way of hitting that nerve. No one could take me out of character like she could.

When I finally managed to make it inside, I kicked my shoes off, threw my keys across the room, and dropped to my knees in tears. I was hurting. I felt broken. I felt lost.

This wasn't the Amina I showed to the world. This

frazzled, blubbering mess who was laid out on my floor was someone I never wanted anyone to see. At that moment, I felt like the insecure little girl my mother chastised for simply being different. Maybe my mom had gotten it right. Maybe I was a fraud. The African and bohemian garb and the peaceful person I embodied outwardly was an image I had conjured up to show to the world. It was a cover for who I was inside. Wasn't it? I was losing myself. I wasn't sure who I was anymore.

I needed to talk to someone. Khalil's name was at the forefront of my mind. I knew it should've been Adebayo, but not only was Khalil my former lover, he was truly one of my best friends. He was whom I wanted in that moment. I wanted to feel his strong arms around me, telling me everything would be okay.

I dialed his number.

After a few rings, he picked up. Wherever he was, it was loud.

"Hey, you sound like you're out. Should I call you back?" I asked.

"Wait … hold on," he said.

I heard his shoes tapping against the concrete as he walked, and the background noise faded. "Hey. Is everything okay?" he asked.

I sighed. "No, not really."

"The girls?"

"No, they're fine. I just came back from my nephew's graduation though, and as usual, *the bitter crew* went in on me."

He was quite familiar with our family dynamic, so he

didn't question who the bitter crew was. "Oh. I'm sorry to hear that."

I was taken aback he didn't say more. He was almost … cold. Normally, he would've gone off on them for going off on me.

We grew unusually silent.

"Well, I was just hoping you had a moment. You know, to help talk me down off the ledge," I mused.

To say the moment was awkward would be an understatement.

His voice became low. "Amina … I'm sorry the night didn't go well, but as I said before, I can't continue being your shoulder to lean on. I mean, when it comes to the girls, of course, I want you to call, but as far as you and me … I can't be the person you call when things go wrong anymore. That's Adebayo's job."

I pulled the phone away and stared at it. I'd heard what he said a few days prior, but a part of me didn't want to believe he was serious. I'd hoped he was just talking out of frustration that day.

My mouth hung open. "But I—"

"Amina, I must move on. *We* need to move on," he said.

"Oh. I didn't know you felt that way."

He sighed. "How could you not? We—"

Before he could continue, I heard a voice in the background. "Khalil … Khalil! Oh, there you are, baby. I didn't want to blow out the candles without you there. What are you doing out here, and who are you talking to?"

I froze.

Hearing a woman call him *baby* didn't feel good. I guess that's how he felt every time he thought about me and Adebayo, but it was what he said next that made me feel like my heart was about to explode.

His voice was distant, and I could tell he was covering the microphone. "Hey, Sydney. Give me a moment, beautiful. I'm going to wrap this call up and I'll be in there shortly."

"Okay. The quicker we finish here, the quicker we can get home so I can give you what I have planned for you tonight," she teased.

"Oh, damn! You're so bad. You best believe I'll be there shortly!" He laughed.

I almost threw up.

"Yeah, so as I was saying …"

"Dang, you don't waste time, huh?" I mumbled, almost inaudibly.

"What was that?" he asked.

"I said no need, Khalil. I got it. I won't bother you again."

"Amina … I … I'm sorry."

"So am I," I answered, then hung up.

Tears streamed down my face. I couldn't believe the era of Khalil and Amina was officially over.

I never made it off the floor that night.

Early the next morning, the essence of burning sage could be detected coming from my home. Too many negatives were plaguing me, and I needed to get some alignment back in my life.

My phone rang several times. Joy was trying to reach me. For a while, I avoided her. I didn't know if I had the wherewithal to deal with her playful energy at that moment. It didn't take long for me to realize, though, that she was just what I needed.

She came to my place. When she showed up, she held up two bags. No doubt filled with some of my favorite things. She hugged me and looked at me pitifully before walking in and setting the bags down on my dining table along with wine and flowers. "You look like shit, my friend, but I got the good stuff. 14.9 proof. In a minute, you won't feel a thing."

I smiled at her weakly. "I appreciate you, girl."

Without saying a word, she went to the kitchen, pulled out two glasses, and proceeded to pop the top of one of the bottles. She poured the drinks, handed me one, got a vase off the counter, filled it with water, and dropped the flowers inside. Then she made her way back over to me, grabbed her glass, and sat across from me.

She took a sip before she asked, "So, what happened?"

I frowned and rolled my eyes. I wasn't excited about rehashing what happened the day before, but I knew speaking about it would be cathartic. "My mother happened. As usual, she found a way to ruin everything. We had a huge blow-up at my nephew's graduation dinner."

Joy grimaced. "Yikes. Bitter Betty strikes again, huh?"

I sipped some more and swiped at my eyes before I unleashed my pent-up frustration. I nodded. "I don't know why I thought this time would be any different. It's just that this was for my nephew, you know?"

"I know. Maybe one day you'll be able to find out what her problem is with you. You two might have to have a sit-down with just—"

I put my hand up. "Don't say it. I don't want to talk about her anymore."

"Okay."

"And that doggone Khalil. He's another one. He doesn't even give a damn. Can you believe he threw me away like a piece of trash?" I asked.

She raised her eyebrows but didn't respond.

"What?" I asked.

"Well …"

"Well, what!" I fussed.

"Well, you kind of didn't give him much to work with, Amina. He's been trying for years. What else did you expect?"

"Well, thanks for your support, friend!"

She turned her palms up to the ceiling. "What? I'm only giving it to you honest and raw. He's a man. Did you want him to wait forever?"

"But what about our friendship? We've always managed to at least speak no matter whom we've dated. Now that *she's* back in the picture, suddenly he doesn't have time for me?"

She shrugged and took another sip. "Maybe he finally realized he *can't* just be your friend anymore."

"I don't need this right now. You're supposed to be on my side!" I pouted.

She said nothing. Instead, she reached inside her purse and pulled out her cigarettes. I watched as she tapped the box before pulling one out and putting it to her lips. I was amazed she would smoke in front of me when I had asked her not to do so just a few weeks prior.

"Joy! What are you doing?" I said.

She reached for her lighter.

"Joy!" I repeated, louder this time.

She flicked the lighter and paused with it up to the cigarette. "Oh, are you ready to hear what I have to say now?" she asked.

I smirked. She was such a jerk. "So, you're just going to smoke in front of me, huh?"

"It's the only way I can get you to listen. Plus, you're driving me to it with all your mess."

I chuckled. "Sorry, I'm just so frustrated, *and* you know I hate those things. I'd appreciate it if you wouldn't ..." I paused. "Actually, never mind, pass that shit."

Her eyes widened, but she did as she was told. She leaned over and lit the cigarette. I took a pull and then coughed a few times.

I stared at it. "Damn, this shit is *nasty*! I don't know how you smoke this stuff."

She laughed then grabbed it and took a few puffs before putting it out.

I got up, found my stash of weed, and went back out to the living room.

Her face lit up when she saw what was in my hands.

"Now, *this* is the good stuff." I laughed.

"Now, that's what I'm talking 'bout, girl!" she exclaimed.

I lit the blunt and we passed it back and forth while we reminisced.

Finally, she said, "Like I was *trying* to say before, my friend, there's going to come a time when you have to choose, even though it seems as if Khalil *might've* made your mind up for both of you."

I hated to hear it, but I needed to. Khalil had been in my life so long; I didn't know how to be without him in some form or another.

"I'm not ready to let him go, though."

She nodded. "I hear you. By the way, what's going on with Adebayo?"

"Let's just say we're hanging on by a thread. He said he needed some space. He's been spending most of his time at his place, and I've only seen him at band rehearsals lately. He feels left out, especially after Khalil called me early the morning after Anisa's birthday party. And I get it. I guess we'll see what happens after our swinger's cruise next weekend though."

"I'm not sure why you're still hanging on to Adebayo, but

do you, boo. We *both* know what's going to happen because he's not Khalil," Joy said.

I sighed and nodded in agreement. "Yeah, he's not Khalil."

She picked my phone up and handed it to me. "Then call him and tell him that before it's too late. Give it one more shot. You know you want that man. Sydney can't hang on to what's not hers."

The sober Amina would probably never have had the guts to call a man who basically said he was done with her, but with Mrs. Weed and Mr. Alcohol, I felt as though I could conquer the world.

Still, my hands shook as I dialed his number. The phone rang twice, but the voice on the other end wasn't his.

"Umm, hello. I'm looking for Khalil?"

"You've reached the correct number," a woman answered. It sounded like Sydney, but I wasn't sure.

At first, I assumed something had happened to him. My stomach became uneasy. "Okay. Is this Sydney? Can you please tell him Amina's on the phone for him?"

She ignored my questions. "Amina, huh?"

"Yes, Amina."

"Hold on."

The line went silent momentarily. When she came back, she said, "He's busy. He says he'll try to get back to you in the next few days."

*Try to get back to me in the next few days?* I thought. That didn't sound like him, but those words let me know he wasn't checking for me like that anymore. He always got right back to me in the past, but then again, in all the years I'd known him, I'd never ever heard a woman answer his phone.

If I'd had any reservations about how he felt about me now, this was my cue that he had moved on and I needed to do the same. "Okay, thanks," I said and hung up.

I closed my eyes and sat back in the chair without a word.

"Well … what happened?" Joy asked anxiously.

"Another woman happened. She just confirmed that that ship has sailed."

There wasn't enough intoxication in the world to fix my broken heart.

# 14

# Love Overboard

When Adebayo and I got to the entrance of the ship for our cruise, we posed hand in hand for photos before we boarded. I was excited about this cruise. I was looking forward to meeting other individuals and shaking things up a bit. I even hoped maybe this would be what we needed to get our relationship back on track, especially since Khalil was nowhere to be found. Maybe one of our trysts would reignite Adebayo to open his mind like when we first started our relationship. Maybe we'd have such a good time, he would want to do that again.

Things started off beautifully with us meeting and greeting other couples who were into *the lifestyle*. Don and Bre was our couple; she was a doctor and he, a teacher. Adebayo and I immediately connected with them. We spent several hours drinking, laughing, and flirting. I was anxious to spend some time alone with Don, who was a hunk of a man. He was tall, intellectual, and *very* into me. Adebayo also looked like he was digging Bre. It was a win-win for all, or so I thought.

After a while, Don leaned over and whispered in my ear that he wanted to spend some time alone with me. I nodded, touching his arm and batting my eyelashes at him. Those were the magic words I'd been waiting for.

He stood up and reached for my hand. I put my hand in his and he pulled me up. I glanced back at Adebayo, who I thought would be following our lead with his newfound friend. But he wasn't. He glared at the two of us.

"Honey, will you and Bre be leaving soon as well?"

He shook his head. "I'm tired. I think I'll just chill."

His reaction made me pause. In fact, it made me uncomfortable. What the hell was his problem? I turned to Don. "Umm, sorry, I don't think this is a good idea. You mind if we take a rain check?"

He looked confused but didn't argue. I got it; you were supposed to swing on a swinger's cruise, or at the least have a little fun with someone other than the person you came with. Adebayo had made this moment uncomfortable for all of us.

The couple left, but I was annoyed with him. And now I had some pent-up frustration I needed to get rid of. I got up and stormed off to our cabin.

When I got to the room, I dug in my bag for my battery-operated boyfriend, then went to the bathroom and turned the shower on. I let the water get as hot as I could take it before I jumped in. The water beating on me felt good, but I wanted more. I lifted my leg and reached for my vibrator. It hummed just right. Just like I wanted it to, just like I needed it to.

I gasped and closed my eyes when it touched my clit, and I bit my lip to keep from moaning too loudly.

The shower door opened. I felt Adebayo behind me as he cupped my breasts and slowly kissed my neck. He took the vibrator from my hands and replaced it with his fingers. I moaned and closed my eyes as he massaged my clit. He dropped to his knees and lifted my leg, resting it on his shoulder. Then he licked my clit until my eyes rolled back in my head.

He stood up. "See, we don't need anyone else, my love. You can have this every night." He planted his lips on mine, and we ravaged each other under the water.

He picked me up, put me against the shower wall, and entered me, then he pounded into me as I screamed. I felt myself on the verge of erupting. My nut was overtaking my senses. "Oh … my … God … Khalil! You feel so good!" I screamed.

I realized my error when he stopped mid-thrust and put me down. He opened the shower door, grabbed a towel, and left the bathroom as I watched in horror.

I took my time in the bathroom before going to bed. Thankfully, he was asleep when I laid beside him.

The next morning, we got up like nothing had happened the night before. He was his old happy-go-lucky self. There were no words exchanged about why he had backed out of hooking up with Bre or my slip-up, and I didn't have the energy to ask.

But then he did the last thing I expected.

At breakfast, he grabbed my hand, got down on one knee and grinned up at me. "Amina, these years together have been a whirlwind of good times and ups and downs, but there's no one else I would rather experience the good, bad, and in-between with. You are a queen and my heart and soul. You are everything I never asked for."

My neck grew hot with embarrassment. I looked out at the crowd nervously and grinned uncomfortably. The sound of chatter and clinking of utensils against plates stopped. The room grew silent as folks watched what was going on.

"What are you doing? Bayo, don't do this," I said through gritted teeth.

He ignored my words. "Amina Thompkins, will you do me the honor of becoming my wife? Will you marry me?"

There were a few gasps and even some whispers as everyone awaited my response. I hated that he put me on the spot, but I wasn't going to let that deter me. I had to stay true to myself. "I ... I ... I can't," I answered, and then I fled.

I ran like I was being chased by the biggest dog. I ran like I was being chased with a gun. I ran from a man I knew loved me more than I deserved to be loved by him.

I took my time making my way back to our cabin simply because I didn't want to see the look of disappointment I'd undoubtedly see on his face.

When I got there, he was already in the room and he didn't say much. In fact, he didn't say anything. He didn't look up from packing his bag.

"Where are you going?" I asked.

He smirked then shook his head before throwing something else into his bag. He barely looked up when he finally spoke. "I was hoping we could move forward together, but just as I thought, you're not ready to move on with me."

I wrung my hands and looked down.

He continued, "Even more so, I don't get why you've been trying to hold on to something you've long since moved on from. This relationship has been over for a long time, and both of us have known that. Stupid me for letting you continue to use me. It doesn't matter anymore though."

I frowned. His words stung. "Don't say that! I thought this trip was about us reconnecting, doing what we do best."

"What we *used* to do best. I told you I'm done with that life. I want all of you or nothing at all."

I went over to him but he raised his hand, stopping me dead in my tracks. I threw my hands up. "But I'm right here. Why do we have to be married for me to prove that to you? Are you sure the real reason you wanted to marry me isn't just so I can have your last name?"

He stopped packing briefly and narrowed his eyes at me. His jaw clenched in anger.

I backed up some. I had gone too far and insulted him.

"Maybe I went about this the wrong way, but I wanted to

see if we had what it took to move forward. If the only thing you can take from me asking you to marry me is about a last name, I'm most definitely doing the right thing."

I looked at him bemusedly. "What do you mean?"

"I wanted to marry you because I *love* you, not for some stupid last name. But it's not the sole reason I chose to ask you on this trip. Maybe in my own little world, I figured if you'd said yes, I'd have known you loved me. I was even willing to look past your little slip-up last night."

I lowered my eyes.

His voice cracked, a subtle clue letting me know he might be holding back tears. "Today has cemented what I've known all along."

"And what would that be?" I asked.

"That there is only one man you would ever marry. One man you'd risk everything to be with. That man is *not* me."

I opened my mouth to speak but couldn't find the words.

He threw the last of his things in his bag. "Exactly."

He was right. Still, my eyes filled with tears at the realization that our lives were about to take on a different course. My well was about to run dry, and I feared what it would look like on the other side. I'd anticipated this moment, but I didn't know it would hurt so bad. It didn't ease the pain of knowing I had hurt him over and over. He was someone I would always care for. He was a good man, he just wasn't *my* man. Despite my best efforts, I couldn't give him what he needed, not when my heart was with someone else.

He came over to me and stared down at me. Then he slowly ran his thumb across my cheek. There was something in his eyes. Something that let me know that, as the song says, this was the end of the road.

"Queen, this is where it ends for me. I can't continue to torture myself. *We* can't continue to torture ourselves. We both deserve better. I reserved another cabin just in case this was the outcome."

He must have *expected* me to say no or he wouldn't have reserved another cabin. He didn't believe in wasting money on things he wouldn't use.

I nodded. There was no use attempting to make someone stay where they didn't feel welcomed. There was no use trying to save what couldn't be saved. Our relationship had run its course. It was time to let go.

Before exiting the cabin, he stopped and turned to me. "Enjoy the rest of the trip. I'll make arrangements to get my things from your place when we get back."

I nodded again.

The next day, I stared out into the choppy blue water as our cruise ship slowly returned to the port of call. I felt slightly nauseated from the movement of the ship, which was a first for me, as I'd cruised on numerous occasions and never had issues previously. The water was extremely rocky, and it echoed my emotions. I had hoped the end of this trip would produce a different outcome, but it came as no surprise that when I disembarked, Adebayo was nowhere to be found.

♫

After a few weeks of no contact, I got the dreaded phone call. As promised, Adebayo made plans to get his things from my place.

I told him to use his key, and I would be there shortly since I was running errands.

Even though I was no longer in love with him, I was sure I wasn't ready to see him removing his things from my place, but I agreed to meet him there in half an hour or so. We had many years between us, so seeing him do so would cement our fate, and I wasn't sure I was ready to deal with that yet.

When I made it to the house, Zion was outside on his phone. He stopped talking when he saw me. "Hello, Miss … I mean, Amina."

After all those years, he still hadn't gotten used to calling me by my first name. I shook my head before I exclaimed, "Hey, Zi! How have you been? I wasn't expecting to see you here."

"I'm well, thanks. Just hanging out with my pops a little today, helping him move some of his things and whatnot." He paused briefly. I sensed he was conflicted on his next words to me. "He's been kind of down since … well, you know."

I nodded my regret. "I understand. Believe me, he's not the only one."

He nodded and walked away to finish his conversation as I spotted Adebayo coming out of the house with a box of his things.

When he saw me, he didn't give away any emotion, but he smiled.

I smiled back.

He looked good. I was glad he didn't look like he felt according to Zion.

"I see Zion's out here keeping you company *instead* of helping his old man," he teased.

Zion laughed and disconnected his phone call. "Got you, Pops. I'll grab another box." He jogged toward the house.

"I tell you, these kids today. I found out recently that he got himself a little girlfriend, so I don't see him much these days. Good help is so hard to find," Adebayo joked.

We both laughed then shared an awkward silence.

"Are you okay … really?" I asked.

He lowered his eyes. "It's going to take some getting used to, but I will be."

"Sorry that things didn't work out, but you don't have to … you know … disappear from my life. We can still be friends beyond our band affiliation. Remember, we were friends first. And I never want things to ever be awkward between us."

"About that …" he began. He stopped short when Zion called him.

"Dad, I don't think there's anything else," he said as he dragged two large bags outside.

"Okay, son. Cool. I'll go and do one last check."

He followed me back into the house and did one final sweep to make sure he hadn't left any of his belongings behind.

I walked him to the front door. Before going outside, he said, "I'll call you at some point. Maybe after I have some time to heal."

I nodded.

"Tell Khalil he's a lucky man," he added. He bent and kissed my cheek before handing me my keys.

I didn't let him know Khalil wasn't checking for me either. I stood in the doorway and watched as he went to his car.

If I thought losing Adebayo would be the extent of my pain, I was sadly mistaken. Khalil and Adebayo exiting my life stage left was just a foreshadowing of things to come.

# 15

# Therapeutic Love

"Whew, it's hot out here. Can we slow down some?" Joy said as she bent over and wiped a bead of sweat from her forehead. It was a few weeks before she was scheduled to leave for Georgia, and we were walking around the lake by my condo. She was so out of breath; if I didn't know any better, I would've thought she had just run a marathon.

I paused and rested my hands on my hips. I wasn't my usual energetic self either. "Yeah, it *is* hot. I'm sure those cigarettes don't help either, but we can slow down if you'd like."

She rolled her eyes. "Whatever. So anyway, do you mean to tell me Adebayo still proposed *after* you called him by another man's name the night before? Your ex-husband, no less. Girl! I *need* to know your secret," Joy exclaimed.

I shrugged. "I'm just being myself, so your guess is as good as mine. What's worse is he proposed at breakfast in front of everyone. I'm sorry I hurt him, and I'm going to miss him, but things played out the way they were supposed to."

She raised her eyebrows, seemingly in awe. "Yeah, that whole situation was a *mess*. So, back to the drawing board, huh?"

I shrugged again. "I don't know. I think I give up. Love sucks. Maybe I should just pick up and move across the country. Or to Africa, Jamaica, or even Italy. I could get myself a Mandingo and run around naked just fuckin' every day."

Joy laughed. "Here you go with that foolishness. My guess is you'd fall in love with several of those Mandingos, and the whole process would start all over again."

"No, I don't think so. I think I'm falling out of love with love. Things get too complicated when you give a damn."

"I can't argue with you on that. Love and I aren't exactly on speaking terms right now either. Especially after all I've been through with this fool. Even so, I think I want to be in love again at some point."

"Really?"

"Of course. Do you see me? There's someone out there that can love *all* of this," she replied as she ran her hands up and down her body.

I laughed. I was glad she was still optimistic about being in love again. I, on the other hand, was not.

We continued walking.

"And regarding you, as long as I've known you, you've always been a lover. You couldn't stop loving if you tried. That's just who you are. Especially that one man whose name starts with a K and ends with il. You can have anyone you want, but you don't ever go too far from him. That's because you two have a special bond."

I grimaced. I didn't want to think about him anymore. I was trying to move on with my life, and I couldn't understand why she wouldn't just let us go.

"You're just feeling sorry for yourself right now. But you're the *one and only* Amina 'Badass.' This ain't you. You'll be back on that horse in no time."

"Yeah, I'm sure I'll be riding something again soon. It might not be a horse though."

We both laughed.

"Honestly, my friend, I think you need to deal with some things before you get serious about anyone again."

I stopped abruptly and grabbed her arm. "Wait … what are you talking about?"

She let out a huge sigh of relief. "Oh, thank God. My ass is tired," she breathed.

I chuckled at her dramatics. "What do you think I need to deal with, Joy?"

"Your childhood. Your daddy dying when you were only seven. I know how bad that hurt you. You never talk about it, *nor* do you want to talk about the issues with your mother."

I put my hands on my hips and closed my eyes.

I remembered the day the police showed up on my door-step to break the news that my daddy had fallen asleep at the wheel and driven headfirst into a semitruck. The paramedics said he probably died before he knew what happened. I was standing behind my mother when we got the news; she gasped and covered her mouth with her hands. I took off, locked myself in the bathroom, and threw myself on the bathroom floor. I curled up in the fetal position and bawled until my throat and mouth felt like sandpaper. She and Jackie had to literally pry the door open and carry me out of the bathroom that evening.

I was a daddy's girl, and he had left me. The first man I ever loved was gone. To add to that, he was the only cushion I had from my mom, and he always believed in my dreams as an artist.

Memories of him made me smile, but they also made me sad. He was an amazing father, but according to my mother, he wasn't the best husband because he always had different women. It didn't matter to me though. My daddy could do no wrong.

I opened my eyes and swiped at them before I began walking again.

Joy huffed as she quickly followed behind me. "See, that's what I mean."

"What do you mean this time?" I said as I hastened to get to the house.

She grabbed my arm, stopped, and forced me to face her. "You barely talk about your father, but you damn sure *won't* talk about your mother."

I threw my hands up in frustration. "What do you want me to say? That she's mean and just pure evil? That nothing

I ever do is good enough for her? All I know is she hates me. She claims her issues with me were because I didn't sing in the church, but I feel there's something more."

"See? That's a great start, my friend. Hate is a *strong* word though. Have you ever asked her *what* her problem is with you? When you think back, could something have happened in your life to constitute a strained relationship?"

"So, now you're my therapist." I was surprised that my usually silly friend could offer up such good advice.

"Nope, just a concerned friend."

I quickly scanned my brain for anything I could remember to sour my relationship with my mother, but I came up with nothing.

"Nope. At first, we had a normal mother-and-daughter relationship. It seems as if one day she just decided she didn't like me and started treating me differently. That's probably one of the reasons I chose to run away with Malcolm in the first place." I paused. "Come to think of it, it may not have been that I was in love with him so much as me wanting to get away from *her*."

Joy nodded and pointed at me. "Bingo. I think you might be on to something."

We began walking again and I stopped to open the front door when Joy said, "One more thing, my friend. I think you should try and make amends with your mom. Talk to her to see if you can understand what her issue is with you."

I immediately got a headache at the idea of doing that. No

matter how old I was, she was still the parent. I didn't want to be the bigger person.

Joy must have sensed my apprehension. "I'm not telling you to force anything, just give it a try. Finding closure on why the two of you are so disconnected could help you figure out why you're struggling so much in the love department. It could be your breakthrough toward healing."

I nodded. "Okay. I make no promises, but I'll see what I can do in the next few weeks."

"That's all I can ask. Remember, sooner than later," she said as she walked in behind me.

I went to the sink, washed my hands, grabbed two bottles of water, and handed her one. "Thanks, Joy. I really needed this."

She nodded. "We can call her now if you'd like."

I glanced at my phone then shook my head. It was too beautiful a day to have my mother mess it up. "Nah, today isn't the day. But maybe you should consider therapy as your next career move. I'd be your first client."

"Whew, my friend. I love you, but there's *not* enough money in the world to deal with all your issues. But I'll be glad to send you some referrals."

# No Love

I looked out at the audience after finishing my first set. "We'll be back in fifteen, so go get you some drinks and don't forget to tip the bartender!" I said and winked at the crowd.

As usual, anytime my band performed, it was a full house. It was often an adrenaline rush to see the eager faces looking back at me while performing, but I wasn't my usual self tonight.

I glanced at the drummer who was replacing Adebayo this evening. I didn't care for him or his drum set. The night felt off without my favorite drummer's presence. I'd wanted space for so long, but now that I got it, it didn't feel so good.

He couldn't face being around me right now, and I got it. I still held out hope that he wouldn't let our relationship ending interfere with his work though.

I sat at the bar alone and ordered a drink. The vodka and cranberry I sipped did little to calm my nerves. I felt the stare from several of my bandmates as they knew I didn't like to drink when I was about to go on. Drinking made my mouth dry, so it was usually a no no for me before a performance.

Tonight was different though. I felt burdened. In just a few short months, my almost-perfect life felt as if it was falling apart.

When I got up to prepare for my next set, I glimpsed a young woman standing at the bar. She appeared to be by herself and had several empty shot glasses lined up beside each other. I watched as she threw a shot back and slammed her glass on the bar table. Then she took another shot. She didn't look happy.

She glanced at me. I smiled at her, but she didn't return my sentiment. Her eyes reminded me of someone, I just couldn't think of who. Although her demeanor was off putting, I wouldn't let that add to the weight I was carrying that night.

I got up on the stage and as usual, sang my heart out. Music was healing. Even better than sex to me. It was the one thing that could take any pain away, so I closed my eyes, threw my head back, and let the music move through me. I felt every note that flowed from my lips. As usual, the crowd cheered after my performance. Their approval was what I needed to lift my spirits.

But, after my second song, as soon as the applause died down, a lone voice could be heard coming from the back of the club. "Boooo! Boooo! You suck! Get off the stage!" the voice bellowed.

In that moment, you could've heard a pin drop.

I opened my eyes and stared in horror at the same woman who had glowered at me moments before. Having someone boo at them was every singer's nightmare. While I couldn't say everyone loved it when I performed, I managed to dodge that bullet in my over-thirty-year career. Until now.

My heartbeat sped up, and my cheeks and neck became hot with embarrassment. If I was lighter-skinned, I would've been red as a beet. The peaceful Amina wanted to dismiss her rudeness, but the embarrassed Amina wanted to kill the bitch. I felt disrespected to my core. If she didn't enjoy the performance, all she had to do was leave.

Several of the patrons turned around to see who the voice was coming from, and several shook their heads. A few of my fans yelled for her to get out. They were obviously disgusted as well.

She was bold. She turned on her heels and walked out of the room.

"We're going to take another fifteen," I said to the audience.

My band members looked at me quizzically. This wasn't our scheduled break.

I mouthed "be right back" over my shoulder and put my microphone down. That was the surefire way to let them know they had no choice.

I hurried away from the stage area to see if I could find the mysterious young woman. I quickly scoured the crowd before making my way into the entryway. When I didn't see her, I went outside. I searched the parking lot as well, but she was nowhere to be found. That was, until I heard a car's tires screech. I spun in the direction of the noise, but all I caught was the back of her head as she fled from the parking lot.

# Dying to Be Loved

A few nights later, an unexpected call interrupted my sleep. My sister's voice was frantic on the other end.

"Amina, she's gone! Mom's gone!"

I yawned and flipped onto my back. Comprehension was slow since I was still waking up. "Gone where, Jackie?"

"She died! She's dead," she screamed.

I sat up abruptly and removed my eyeshades. Even though she was blubbering, this time I was sure I'd heard correctly.

"What do you mean, she died? She was fine when I saw her a few days ago!"

Jackie ignored my slow cognition and got straight to the point. "Just get here! Kareem and I are at her house!" she screamed before the phone disconnected.

I rolled out of bed and went to the bathroom. My legs and arms felt heavy as I washed my face and brushed my teeth. I didn't know how to feel as I summoned a rideshare. I wasn't happy, but I couldn't say I was sad. What I was, was numb, zombielike … lifeless. Just going through the motions. Was my mother really gone? This moment didn't seem real.

The thirty-minute ride to the house felt longer than it should have. After getting out of my ride, I stood frozen in place. It felt strange, standing in front of my family home. The place looked eerily the same except for the parts of the house that needed to be touched up with paint. I felt a tinge of guilt for not doing more for my mother. No matter how difficult she had been, I could've tried harder.

Kareem was standing outside. He hugged me tight and opened the door for me to go in. I was relieved to find the coroner had already removed her body from the premises because no matter what kind of relationship we had, I wouldn't have felt comfortable seeing her like that.

When I spotted Jackie, I immediately felt pity for her. She still had on her hair bonnet along with her night clothes. My usually well-put-together sister was a wreck, and for good reason. She had lost her best friend.

Thankfully, Kareem's father and my daughters Anisa and Talia were already there to offer comfort.

When Jackie saw me, she ran over and threw herself into my arms. This was a different Jackie. I was always used to her being so hard. It was a testament to spending too much time in my mother's presence.

"What happened?" I asked once I was able to pry her off me.

She looked up at me with puffy eyes. "I'm not sure. They say she went in her sleep. She'd been complaining that she wasn't feeling good for weeks now."

"Wow. I wish you would've told me," I said.

My sister looked me up and down like I'd lost my mind. "Would it have mattered?"

Jackie was correct. I opened my mouth but had no rebuttal. Other than suggesting my sister take her to see a doctor, I didn't know how much I would've done. My throat tightened and my heart felt heavy. My eyes filled with tears. How could I have allowed my relationship with my mother to come to this? I claimed to be a lover. I had no excuse to not give love to the woman who had birthed me.

Jackie shook her head furiously and backed away from me. She threw her hands up. "Don't cry now. You never cared about her. I hope you're happy," she yelled as she covered her face and ran from the room.

I began to follow her but my daughters stopped me.

"Give her space, Iya. She needs some time," Talia said.

I nodded and was thankful to see Kareem and his father go after her. I hoped they could give her what I could not.

A week and a half later, we stood around my mother's grave. I was frozen in place, feeling a range of emotions. Honestly, I wasn't sure how I should feel. While she wasn't always the best mother to me, I knew she loved me in her own way.

I was a singer who couldn't sing at my own mother's funeral because I was too ashamed. Thankfully, my daughter Anisa was able to do it for me. For those who didn't know my mother or the strenuous relationship we had, it wouldn't matter. Those people probably assumed I was in too much pain to make it through a song, so I knew it wasn't even a second thought.

Khalil and Adebayo had also shown up for me. Adebayo sat to my left, and Khalil to my right. When a lone tear fell from my eye, Adebayo grabbed my hand and squeezed it. Khalil put his arm around my shoulders, and I slightly leaned on him. I caught Adebayo's eye as he glanced in our direction, but thankfully whatever emotions he had, he kept them to himself.

My heart felt heavy. Especially knowing she had died alone. No matter how fractured our relationship had been, no one deserved to die without someone holding their hand. What especially haunted me, though, was the fact that I would never get the chance to gain closure with her.

The service was amazing, and it was even good to see some of the same church folk who didn't like me as a child. I selfishly relished in the fact that I had turned out much better than they thought I ever could.

As I was leaving the graveside, I glanced at someone staring in my direction from behind one of the trees. She quickly turned on her heels when she realized she'd been made. I recognized her immediately. It was the young heckler from the club the other night. What the hell was she doing here? To say I was upset that she'd have the nerve to show her face here was an understatement, especially on a day like today.

I went to confront her but was stopped by several of the other mourners. This was a public funeral, so I wasn't surprised she knew where the service was. I hated that Jackie didn't listen to me in keeping that information confidential. The thought of hiring security ran through my mind as I wondered if I had a stalker on my hands.

I tried my best to acknowledge and thank the mourners as I didn't want to be rude, but I couldn't concentrate on them. I looked over their shoulders and spun around, frantically looking for the woman. I didn't want her to disappear on me again. But, as feared, she was nowhere to be found.

When Joy saw I was still standing there scouring the graveyard, she came over to me.

"Hey, are you okay?" she asked.

It was then I realized I hadn't done a good job of disguising that something was going on. Several of the attendees stopped and stared at me as I spun around in circles. "Yes. I'm sorry. I thought I glimpsed an unwanted familiar face."

Joy was on it. "Oh, really? Who? Where are they?" she asked and began to scan the crowd as well.

I didn't want to cause a scene. "I'll tell you later, girl," I said as I reluctantly walked away. I kicked myself for letting her escape ... again.

# 18

# Vengeance, not Love

"Excuse me? Can you please repeat that, Renee?" I asked my accountant for the third time.

I had received her urgent call during brunch with my daughters and rushed right over to her office afterward. It was rare that she called me, so I was taken aback when she'd asked that I come in immediately. Thankfully, her office wasn't far from where we were because I was a wreck. Honestly, driving was probably the last thing I should've been doing at that moment.

She adjusted her glasses and stared into the computer again. "Yes, ma'am. Okay, so, there doesn't appear to be enough money in this account to cover your mortgage or other bills this month."

I blinked and scratched my head. "That's impossible. I just transferred twelve thousand dollars last month, and that's to add to what was *already* in there."

She nodded. "And that's why I called you. I knew

something had to be wrong because I've never seen your funds so low. You always have enough funds to cover your bills."

She had to be mistaken. There was no way the money wasn't in that account.

"Let me check it myself," I said. I pulled my phone out and opened my bank account on my app. The app reflected what my accountant had just said. I had only five hundred dollars in my account. The rest of the money had been drawn out over the course of the last several days. I kicked myself for not allowing the notifications to my phone from the bank. Normally I would have been on top of this myself, but with so much going on in my life lately, I'd been slippin'.

I did a quick mental tally of all the bills connected to that account. I knew I wasn't losing my mind.

"Excuse me, I'll be right back," I said.

I stepped into the lobby and called the bank. The woman on the other end didn't have much information except to ask if I remembered transferring a large portion of the money to an account with an Adebayo Okafor and Amina Thompkins.

"Wait, what? Miss, I can promise I haven't transferred any money to that account recently."

"You *are* Amina Thompkins though, correct?"

"Yes, I am. How much did you say was transferred again?"

From the way she sounded on the phone, I quickly deciphered she was chewing gum. I heard her fingers tapping the keyboard. She reminded me why some people didn't belong in customer service.

"I didn't say, but from my records, I see fifteen thousand dollars."

My eyebrows rose as my stomach churned with anger. "That doesn't make sense."

"So, you're saying you didn't transfer any money to yourself?" she asked.

I didn't like her tone. Now it sounded as if I was lying, and with so much going on in my life, I began to doubt myself. Before I decided to launch a full-on investigation though, I decided maybe I should do some additional checking. I figured it might be hard to prove theft since my name was still linked to the account.

"Like I said before, I didn't transfer any money to that account recently, but please cancel the debit cards linked to the account."

"I would need *both* parties to authorize that," she answered.

I took a deep breath. *Dammit!* "Okay. Well, please do not allow any more transactions until I get this sorted out. I need to check something and get back to you shortly," I ordered.

"Would you like us to open an investigation in the meantime?" she asked.

I thought about her question. Adebayo's face appeared in my mind. It was him. It had to be. But how? Why? I felt a mixture of rage and hurt that someone who claimed to love me would take advantage of me like this. I had so many questions. Was he still upset about our breakup? Was he doing this for revenge because of all I had put him through during our relationship? I needed answers before I reported him.

"Not yet. Give me a couple days to get back to you."

"Okay, sounds good. We'll be awaiting your phone call," she answered.

I rolled my eyes. *Yeah, right.*

I opened my bank app again and checked to see if what she had said was correct.

Sure enough, I saw the date the funds were transferred as well as when the money was taken out of the account. I didn't know how I was going to prove that I didn't transfer or withdraw those funds. I kicked myself for not closing out the account we had together immediately. I'd been dealing with so many things as of late, it had slipped my mind.

I retreated into Renee's office and sat down.

She could clearly tell I was disturbed. "Are you okay, Mrs. Thompkins? I can only imagine how upsetting this must be for you. I have some information for private investigators I can pass along, if you need it."

"Thanks. I think I know who did this, but I'll take the information just in case. I promise I'm going to get to the bottom of this one way or another."

She opened her drawer and pulled out a folder. She thumbed through it, then wrote down several numbers and handed them to me.

"I'll be in touch shortly. Let me check a few things out first." I took the information and put it in my bag then left, my mind reeling.

# A Confusing Love

When I got home, I dropped my things and headed straight to my closet where the safe was. I moved my clothes aside as I scoured the room for any clues or anything out of place. Since my closet was meticulous, I knew where everything was. I would've been able to pinpoint if anything had been moved. As I combed through my belongings, I racked my brain to think of anything that would make sense about how Adebayo would've gotten my bank information.

Nothing seemed out of place.

I opened the safe and checked its contents. The debit card, checkbook, and account information to my and Adebayo's account was missing.

I fingered the paper Renee had given me. She was right; I would have to call in the big dogs to get the answers I needed.

The sun barely rose before the investigator made it to my

house the next morning. He couldn't have been older than thirty and was dressed in street clothes: baggy pants and a button-down shirt. He did his due diligence and went over the specifics with me.

As we sat at my dining table and I explained how my money had mysteriously been transferred out of my account to a joint account, I felt unnerved.

He pulled out an iPad to take my information. "Did you check with your daughters since they have access to your home and the safe?" he asked.

I watched him as he typed on the iPad. This was different. I was old-school—pen and pad. It was uncomfortable sharing my information with a complete stranger. I questioned how much experience he'd had doing this and if he knew what he was doing. Could I trust him with my personal information?

"Absolutely. Like me, they have no clue what could have happened. Besides, the money was transferred to my and my ex's joint account."

"What computer do you make your deposits/withdrawals from?"

I got up and brought my laptop over to him. "Sometimes I use my phone, but most of the time, I use this laptop."

"Do you mind if I inspect it?"

"Please do."

I turned it on and watched as he scrolled through my web pages, email, and any and everything he could possibly find on my screen. Then, he turned the computer over and opened whatever he could.

"Okay. It doesn't look like you have a virus or have anything that could have been downloaded to your hard drive. So, this safe you mentioned."

"It's in my closet."

"Mm-hmm. If you don't mind, might I ask what is in the safe?"

My body stiffened. "It has banking information, debit and credit cards, some cash, and a host of other personal information. As I've said before, the only people who have access to that information are my daughters."

He nodded. "Okay. Do you mind if I see your closet?"

I nodded hesitantly and got up. "Please follow me."

I was pretty sure he wouldn't find anything in there because I'd already scoured the closet's contents plenty of times. I stood back and watched as he did the same thing I had done the day before.

He moved my clothes, shoes, and everything he could find. Fifteen minutes later though, he looked up at the ceiling. He reached up and unscrewed the light bulb, then he pulled his phone out and turned his flashlight on. I watched as he inspected it for a few moments. He emerged from the closet like he'd just won a prize.

"I think this might be the culprit. It appears to be a spy camera." He handed it to me.

My eyes bulged. Especially when I realized the bulb wasn't the high-efficiency one I used to save energy.

I took the light bulb from him and inspected it thoroughly. To say I was mortified that someone could have done this to me would be an understatement. This thing had been in my home where I had private moments. It was in my domicile where I shared my secrets and walked around naked.

I was incensed.

"Can you find who planted this?" I asked.

He nodded. "Give me a few days. I'll see if it can be linked to an IP address, but they make these things so advanced these days, I still may not be able to get anything from it. One quick suggestion though. You might want to consider getting some security cameras."

That's the one thing I should've listened to Adebayo about: getting those damn security cameras installed.

"I'm on it. I'll be calling them as soon as you leave. I think I already know who did this though, I just needed confirmation. Thanks for your help."

As soon as he left, I dialed Adebayo's number and paced the room as I waited for him to answer. My blood was boiling. That thin line between love and hate reared its ugly head, and it was taking everything in me not to report him to the authorities. What I really wanted to do was hurt him. Physically and mentally.

"Stupid! Stupid! Stupid!" I fussed. I was angry at myself for not being more proactive about taking care of this bank stuff sooner. Other than my mother's funeral, I hadn't had much interaction with Adebayo since he moved his things from my home. When I did try to speak with him, he'd been short. It had to be him. It was the only thing that made sense.

When he didn't answer the first time, I sent a text that it was urgent and called him again. Surprisingly, this time, he answered.

"Hey, do you have a moment? I have something urgent to speak to you about."

He sighed. "Amina. I asked for some space, I—"

I didn't let him finish. "It's not that. I understand that things have been tense between the two of us lately, but I never thought it would come to this."

"Come to what?" He seemed genuinely lost.

He wasn't going to appreciate what I had to say next, but I didn't care. "I know I hurt you and things are tough on you financially, but that doesn't make it okay for you to take from me. All you had to do was ask. I would've given you back your money from our account. I would've lent you some of mine as well if you really needed it," I spat.

"Wait … what are you talking about?"

"The money in my account, Adebayo. You stole from me. You planted a device in my closet to spy on me, then transferred money from my account to our joint account, then went to the bank and withdrew the funds."

He blew out air. "What? Amina, you're not making sense.

I don't even know how to get in your safe. Did you check with the bank? Maybe there's an error."

"Of course I did. They were the first ones to let me know the money was transferred into our account. Then it was withdrawn from that same account. You obviously knew how to transfer my money, and you got the information from somewhere. Was it that time I asked you to let the workmen in? Did you conspire against me and split the profits with the workers?"

"What?"

"This is what happens when you let people into your personal space," I spat. I trusted you! You were the only one besides my girls who had access to my home. I remembered you snuck up on me when I was in the safe that time. Were you looking then?"

"Wow ... really?" he huffed.

"Yes, really!" I shot back.

"Do you hear yourself? You should know me better than that. First of all, I would *never* steal from you, and again, even if I wanted to, which I don't, I have *no access* to your accounts. You have *all* the information for our joint account. I even gave you my debit card."

"The debit card and checkbook is missing too," I said lowly.

"What ... how? I don't understand."

"I don't know! That's why I'm asking you!" I yelled. I covered my face with my hand and shook my head. I didn't feel good about accusing him, but there was no other explanation.

The line became silent and I thought he may have hung up.

Finally, he asked, "Are you sure there's not something you're missing?"

"I've called my children, the bank, and now you. Somebody's lying, and I'm pretty sure it's not my kids or the bank."

"So, that's it. You're resolute that I had something to do with this?"

I rubbed my temples when I felt a migraine coming on.

"Wow! After all the years we spent together, you really don't think much of me, huh?"

"It's not that. It's just that nothing in my life is making sense anymore!"

I took a few deep breaths and closed my eyes. I needed to take a beat and think. It wasn't adding up. Adebayo was a lot of things, but he wasn't a thief. I was jumping way ahead of the gun. Besides, why would he have been bold enough to answer my call if he'd stolen from me?

Empathy was etched in his voice when he spoke again. "I hear you, and I'm sorry you've been going through so much lately, but it'll be okay soon enough. Let me check some things on my end and I'll get back to you in a few days. I'm still here for you if you ever need to … you know … talk."

I nodded as my eyes filled with tears. "I appreciate that."

# 20

# Betrayed by Love

"Hey, Auntie A," Kareem said when I walked through the door. "You should check your Instagram. Your page is now verified!"

Things were finally dying down after my mom's funeral, so my sister and I thought it would be a good time to go through Mom's things. The thought of doing so was making me nauseous, so I wasn't necessarily in a rush to find Jackie.

My brow wrinkled in confusion. "Um, can I please get my hug? And what does that mean exactly?"

While I might've been forward in my thinking and was "the cool auntie," as the kids would say, I didn't do my own posting on social media. I had a social media manager for that. Besides, with the way things were going in my life lately, social media was the least of my concerns.

He laughed before reaching down and giving me a tight

hug. "It means you're official. You know ... like your page is legit," he said.

"Oh. Okay." I still didn't fully comprehend what he was putting down. I was thankful to have young people in my life to keep me on track though.

"No cap, Auntie. This is big! You should check it when you get a chance. In fact, unlock your phone and let me see it."

"No what?" I asked, but I didn't have the energy to try and learn another slang term. I shook my head. "Never mind." I handed him my unlocked phone. No matter how young I looked, these kids always reminded me of my age.

Within seconds, he had my page pulled up. He pointed to the checkmark beside my username. "See, Auntie? This blue check by your profile name. That's what I was talking about. It should be great exposure for your album and whatnot too."

"Oh, nice. I tell you, this social media stuff is a blessing and a curse, but every little bit helps. Thanks, nephew."

"You're welcome."

"Where's your mom?"

He shrugged. "She was in Grandma's room last I checked."

"Okay. I'll make sure to come see you before I leave," I said before heading in the direction of my mother's room. I figured it was best I got it over with rather than drag it on any longer.

I slowly made my way down the hall. When I got to my old room, I paused and peeked in. Memories came flooding back. No matter how tough things had been between my mother and I, I still had some good memories here. I spotted my favorite rocking chair in the corner, went over to it, and sat down. I closed my eyes and rocked back and forth. I was exhausted. Peaceful rest had been evading me lately.

Sleep washed over me. In an instant, the face of the mysterious woman who had been tormenting me appeared. Unfortunately, she'd been showing up in my dreams. Pun intended—she had become a nightmare. "You think you're just so perfect, huh?" she said.

"What are you talking about?" I asked.

"I'm talking about *you*. You're a fraud. You *can't* sing that well, that's why I had to boo you, nor are you the good person you claim to be. You hurt people. You ruin families."

I was questioning everything about myself lately. Maybe I didn't sing as good as I thought I did. Her booing me at the club the other night did have me questioning my singing abilities. I put my hands on my hips and lifted my chin as I pretended her words didn't faze me.

"I won't let you take that from me. I'm a legend! You're trying to take over thirty years of me being a bomb-ass singer away from me. I *know* I can sing. I love to sing. It's what I was *born* to do."

She rolled her eyes and scoffed. "If you say so."

I crossed my arms. "Whatever! You're wrong about me. I'm not perfect, but I would never intentionally hurt anyone. I would never ruin anyone's family. That's not who I am. I *try* to be a good person."

"Well, you're not! Your own mother didn't even like you,

and now, you've driven away the men who loved you. All because you can't commit to one. In fact, that's what you do best. You scare away anyone who dares to love you. Even your daddy left. You're not getting any younger either. One day, no one is going to want you when your ass is old and dried up. Most of us would kill to have someone love us, and you had two men willing to be with you forever and that *still* wasn't enough," she yelled.

"But Malcolm couldn't be monogamous, and my ex-husband had a slip-up as well. As wonderful as my daddy was, even he cheated. Men can't be monogamous. No one can. No matter how much love two people have between them. It's just not normal for humans to be that way."

She rolled her eyes. "Are you serious? You had a perfectly good man in Adebayo, but you didn't want him. Besides, we humans have the right to choose. Isn't that what you tell your children? People make mistakes. That's what makes us human. God knows you've made quite a few yourself. You're just selfish. You don't deserve love. That's why everyone has left you. You're going to die old and alone just like your mother!"

"Don't say that. I'm *not* selfish. I do deserve love. Everyone does! Wait ... I don't have to answer to you. Why are you even here?"

She laughed sadistically. "I'm going to expose you. I'm going to expose you for all that you *are*, and all that *you're not*."

"Amina? Amina? Are you okay?" Jackie said.

I opened my eyes to find myself drenched in sweat. I couldn't believe I'd fallen asleep that quickly. That dream felt real. Too real.

"I was looking for you. Are you here to sleep or help me go through Mom's things?" she mused.

"Sorry, sis," I said as I got up and followed her back to my mother's room.

Although I was dreading what we had to do, I somehow hoped this might help Jackie and I grow closer. Maybe this could be a bonding moment between sisters. Grief tended to draw folks together in certain situations. Why couldn't our moment be the same?

And it was special, at first.

In Mom's room, there were boxes everywhere. Thankfully, Jackie had already begun the tedious task of packing up our mother's things.

I went through several of the boxes. One held most of our family photos. One of the first photos I spotted was a picture of me and Jackie as children. Happy memories of our childhood flooded my thoughts. I remembered that day like it was yesterday. We were all smiles. We looked like we liked each other. It was way before the bullshit in life made it complicated.

"Remember this?" I asked, holding up the picture of the two of us arm in arm.

It was after church, and we had on our little red dresses. She was slightly taller than me. It was one of the many occasions where my mother had dressed us alike. I had forgotten how close we were at one time and how even though we didn't resemble each other, we took pride in letting folks know we were sisters. We each had two pigtails with white clips: two in the front, and one in the back. We had on white socks that reached our knees, with black shoes.

Jackie came over and took the picture from my hands. She shook her head and laughed out loud, clearly reminiscing as well. "You couldn't tell us we weren't the shit."

I echoed her laugh. "Ain't that the truth!"

We continued to look through photos and reminisce, until I got to a picture at the bottom of the box. Our mom was sitting in a man's lap, and a young Jackie was standing beside them. I looked closer. The man wasn't our father. I flipped the picture over to check the date it was taken.

1973. It was enough for me to know I was around three, Jackie was seven, *and* our father was still very much alive at the time.

"Who's this?" I asked.

Immediately, her smile turned into a frown. "Where did you get that? Give it to me."

I wasn't having it. I was taller than her, so I had no issues holding the picture out of her reach. "Not until you tell me who this man is!"

"It doesn't matter."

"Obviously it does if you can't tell me."

"It's probably best if you don't know."

"Jackie … I want to know now!"

She took a deep breath and rolled her eyes before backing down. She turned her back to me. "He's my father."

I was dumbfounded. She wasn't making sense, and I wasn't in the mood for games. "Jackie, look at me. What do you mean?"

She turned and slowly faced me. Her shoulders slumped. She appeared to be carrying the weight of the world, and she lowered her voice. "You heard me. The man in the picture is *my* father and mom's one true love, according to her."

It felt like the air was sucked out of the room. My eyes widened as I stepped back and put my hands on my head.

"*Your* father? Jackie, we have the same father. Dad is *your* father. I don't understand."

She took a deep breath and spoke with her hands. "I'm not sure what you can't comprehend. Amina, look at the picture. Look at him. Look at me."

I did as I was told and took a closer look. She was right. She looked just like him down to the light skin and freckles. I stared at her but couldn't speak. All along, the two of them shared that huge secret, but never shared it with me. My heart was broken.

"I still don't understand. How?" I asked no one in particular.

"Mom cheated on *your* father with mine. *You* were a product of that."

"But why did she marry my father if she didn't love him?" I asked.

Jackie sat on our mother's bed. She looked worn … tired. I suppose keeping a secret this long could do that to a person.

"The only reason Mom married your dad is because she was forced by her mother. Back then was a different time, and our grandmother was fully involved in the church. She wouldn't let our mother continue to have children and be unwed. Mom never loved him though. She told me all the time. She always said she wished she never met him."

My eyes filled with tears. If she hadn't met him, there would be no me. It was slowly becoming clear why she seemed to carry resentment for me.

"Well, what happened to your father?"

"He moved on and got remarried after you were born. We didn't hear from him for years. Then, we heard he had passed away from cancer."

My mother had lost the love of her life, and Jackie had lost her father too. It didn't make it right, but it gave some insight as to why my mother was so bitter.

"Is that why she treated me the way she did? Why she always treated me like … like … she hated me?" I barely managed to get out.

She shrugged. "I don't know. Probably."

I stared into space because I couldn't speak.

Instead of doing what most sisters probably would do and offering comforting words or at least a hug, Jackie added fuel to the fire. "I guess you two are more alike than you thought, huh?"

Her words pierced my soul. For one of the few times in my life, I became speechless. If she'd wanted to hurt me, she'd succeeded. I didn't know what to do, so I did what I did best: I hurried out the door, jumped into my car, and sped off without looking back.

# Love of Scandal

"Damn, my friend. You've been through pure hell these past few months! You don't deserve that. I don't even want to imagine how you felt when you saw that picture," Joy said groggily. I had just finished giving her the rundown of what happened at my mother's house the night before. It was still early, so I was glad she had answered my call. I was even happier that she was willing to listen to my drama. She had left for Georgia a few weeks before, but with all that had been going on lately, I needed my friend.

After Jackie's revelation, sleep was evading me. I had jumped in my car early the next morning, turned my radio up, and drove. I didn't know where I was going, I just needed to get away. I was literally driving down the lonely highway in hopes of escaping the inescapable and trying to do the impossible:

I was running from myself. I was adrift in the sea of lies and betrayal. Nothing was making sense anymore.

I had so many questions. If my own mother and sister could lie to me this long, who could I trust? If someone could come into my home and plant a camera on me, who could I trust? If someone could steal from me, who could I trust? If Khalil didn't think I was worth fighting for anymore, who could I trust? I glanced at myself in my rearview mirror and didn't recognize the person looking back at me. How had I gotten here?

The Universe was chewing me up and spitting me out. I felt like a scorned stepchild, like a fish out of water.

"It's not even that we have different fathers, I just don't understand why they never told me that information. She hated my father, and she took it all out on me. I had nothing to do with her decisions."

My phone clicked, signaling I had an incoming call on the other line. I glanced at it and saw Jackie's name flash across the screen. I didn't want to talk to her in that moment, so I silenced it.

"You're right. It's unfair, but unfortunately, a lot of mothers take out their hatred for the father on their children. It happens more than you know," Joy said.

My song began to play on the radio, and my mood was transformed. People were loving my single. It never got old hearing my voice on a track. At least something was going right. Music was the one thing no one could take from me.

"Joy, you hear that? They're playing my song!" I exclaimed.

"Yep. Turn that shit up!" she said.

And that's just what I did. Joy and I sang along with the track. But my high didn't last. As soon as the song ended, I heard …

"Stay tuned. After the break, we'll bring you the scandal of the week. We're about to give the tea on how singer-songwriter Amina Thompkins got caught in a real-life homewrecking scandal."

My breath caught in my throat, and I tried to concentrate on keeping the car on the road as I fought to keep my composure. It was surprising that my publicist hadn't warned me about this as she was usually on point about keeping ahead of scandals. Something like this could ruin everything I had worked so hard for.

"Joy, I'll call you back," I said.

"What happened? Is everything okay?" she asked.

"I just need a moment. I'll call you back!" I disconnected the call.

I figured I must've heard wrong. After the agonizing two-minute commercial break and against my better judgment, I turned the radio up and waited to hear what mess they could've possibly uncovered about me.

Jameson: "Chile, y'all ain't gonna believe this tea about Amina 'Badass' Thompkins I have for you today!"

Angel: "Oh shoot. Tell me more, boo!"

Mel: "Do you mean the same Amina that was on our show not too long ago?"

Jameson: "Yes, Mel, you heard right. *That Amina honety* … The person wanted to remain anonymous, but they're accusing Amina of breaking up their happy home years ago. They said, and I quote, 'Don't believe that front she puts on. She's fake. She wouldn't know love if it slapped her in her face.' The person also says their family still hasn't been able to recover from the pain Amina has caused."

Angel: "Dang, that's messed up. I did hear she's into open relationships and that swinging lifestyle."

Jameson: "Yep. I mean she's gorgeous and all, but chile, don't y'all think she's a little too old to be out here breaking up homes? Doesn't she have grandkids and whatnot?"

Angel: "Whew, chile! I know that's right! She needs to sit her ass down somewhere."

Mel: "I mean, can you blame ole boy though? She's probably wrecked quite a few homes in her heyday, looking the way she does. Most fifty-something-year-olds don't look like that! Plus, the woman said this happened years ago. Maybe she's changed. In my book, she can still get it. Amina, if you need to, you can cry on my shoulder any time."

Angel: "Mel, you need help."

Mel: "I'm just saying, she ain't Angela Bassett, but dammit, she might be close. Her body is bangin' and she could pass for someone ten years younger. Talk about aging gracefully! My question would be, why would this person come forward now if this happened years ago? What are they hoping to gain?"

Jameson: "That's a good question. I hate to have to talk

about her because she's a nice lady, but that won't stop this tea from getting spilled! Amina … honey, if you're listening, nothing personal. I'm just doing my job and giving these people what they want! Yassss!" he added as if it was supposed to make me feel better.

Unfortunately, I had heard right. My private life had become public. Tears welled up in my eyes and damn near blinded me as they threatened to fall. It hadn't even been three full months since I was on this morning show, and now they were talking about me like a dog. Even worse, I couldn't believe they would do this right after they played my own song. What an insult!

The ridiculous part was I wasn't sure whose home I had wrecked. If this was ten, fifteen years ago, maybe I could've cracked down on who made this kind of accusation. All I knew was my past was catching up with me.

In any case, Jameson was right. He was a shock jock, this *was* what they got paid for, and my story was no different. I felt embarrassed, and for one of the first times in a long time, I felt alone. This might have been the straw to break the camel's back. Jameson and his band of gossiping disc jockey bandits were probably right … maybe I *was* getting too old for this. My lifestyle was starting to catch up with me.

My phone began to ring off the hook, no doubt with calls from my daughters checking on me, but at that moment I was too ashamed to answer. I was also too choked up to talk.

This wasn't supposed to be my life. My tears were obscuring my vision. I pulled off to the side of the road to get myself together. I grabbed several tissues, blotted my eyes, and blew my nose. I took a few deep breaths to compose myself then called my publicist.

She answered on the first ring. I didn't have to say much.

"Dana, have you been listening to the radio? What's—"

"Ms. Thompkins, I'm already on it. I'll let you know what I find out shortly."

I nodded and disconnected the line. There wasn't much else that needed to be said. I'd done my share of dirt in my years of being in this business, but I'd always managed to escape scandal. I prided myself on that, so this wasn't something I was prepared to deal with. Especially when I was *just* getting back into the music game. I was surprised that now when I wasn't even dating much, something like this would come up.

My phone rang again. It was Anisa. Even though I didn't feel like talking, my daughter was an attorney, so I figured she could give me some advice on how to move forward.

I pulled back onto the road and made my way to her home.

I knocked twice and entered. My daughter's voice could be heard from upstairs. "Come up, Iya. I'm on the patio."

I went upstairs, then opened her sliding door. She had her legs propped up and was sipping on some lemonade. "What, no wine?"

"I'm good right now, but you know I keep wine on deck. Do you want some?"

I sure could've used several drinks at that moment but decided to chill. "Maybe later."

"Okay."

I sat in the chair beside hers and crossed my legs. "Why aren't you at work?"

She took a deep breath, rolled her eyes, and leaned her head in the chair. "I figured I'd go in a little late today. It's such a beautiful day; I wanted to enjoy a few moments of this weather and take a moment to think before I went in and had to deal with all the drama. Plus, I have a lot of thinking to do regarding Terrence."

"Oh, do you now? What are you thinking of regarding him and what drama are you referring to?"

"Well, Iya, honestly, I'm thinking that I may be on the tail end of being a lawyer. I'm not sure if this is for me anymore. And, as far as Terrence, I don't know. Something is just off with him. I told him about my job, and you know what he said?"

I pulled my sunglasses down and stared over them at her. "What did he say?"

"He said, and I quote, 'Sometimes we have to put up with certain things to get where we need to go.' It's like his ass didn't even give a damn."

My eyes widened, but I wasn't surprised. He was slowly showing his true colors, just like I thought he would.

"And as far as work is concerned, a lot of negative stuff has been happening at the firm. Things that are making me realize I shouldn't be there. I'm not sure what I'll be doing yet, but I'll figure it out."

I nodded. Maybe my dream of her leaving her corporate job would come true sooner than I anticipated. My daughter was so talented, there was no doubt she would soon be ready to make her mark on this world. I smiled on the inside at her discovery.

"Well, good for you. Keep me posted," I said.

"Will do." She changed the subject. "By the way, I'm sorry about what they said about you on the radio earlier today. I heard everything."

I nodded and pulled my sunglasses up. I didn't want her to see how upset the incident was making me. I'd been a master at disguising my emotions from my children, and I wasn't about to stop now.

"That's something I wanted to talk to you about. This could hurt me reestablishing my career. You think I should sue for defamation of character?"

My phone rang. If it was anyone other than my publicist, I might not have answered. "One sec. Let me get this," I said before I hit the answer button.

Unfortunately, her findings weren't what I wanted to hear. "The information that the radio show got came from *an anonymous, but trusted source*," she confirmed.

"Well, if they can share my information, why is it okay for them to remain anonymous? How is that fair?"

"I know you're upset, but try not to worry too much. I'm going to follow up with my source. If they find something, anything at all, I'll let you know."

"Okay, thanks for checking." I hung up, but her call didn't relieve my anxiety. In fact, it heightened it.

"Everything okay?" Anisa asked.

I shook my head. "No, not at all. So, about that defamation of character lawsuit," I began as I closed my eyes and rested my head back on my chair.

"Well, first things first, you want to make sure whoever told your story really doesn't have a leg to stand on. I mean, you've *really* lived, Iya. Think back. It could be *anyone*, and it could be true with the lifestyle you've had. Relationships already aren't easy, and I imagine dating more than one person at a time definitely has its own set of challenges."

I nodded. She wasn't lying.

She paused and looked up. "Hmm, but the more I think about it, this might actually help your career."

"What do you mean?" I asked.

"Celebrities deal with this stuff all the time. Sometimes they even create a scandal when they have a movie or album coming out to generate attention. You know how it goes. You may not like it, but since your album is about to drop soon, the timing of all this is perfect."

"Wow, people still do that mess?"

"They sure do. It's probably even worse now *because* of social media. This whole thing will blow over before you know it though. With the time and money it would take to file a defamation lawsuit, you'd be better off using that toward more press. This will probably boost your sales on the streaming platforms before it hurts them. Trust me."

I didn't like it, but at that moment, I decided to trust what my daughter was saying. Especially when I had so many other things to worry about. Like figuring out how to get my life back on track.

# Love to the Rescue

was on my way out the door to go to rehearsals when my phone rang. Adebayo's name flashed across the screen.

I was surprised he would be calling me at this time since he knew the band schedule.

I almost didn't answer, but I figured I could quickly direct him to another time to talk.

"Hey, Bayo, do you mind if—"

"Amina, can I meet you at the bar after you finish rehearsal today? I have something to share about the bank stuff we discussed the other day."

The words *bank stuff* immediately moved his call to the utmost importance, so I didn't argue. "Okay, sure. Is everything okay?"

"Oh, it's about to be. See you soon," he answered and hung up.

I was so consumed with Adebayo's words that I could

barely concentrate during rehearsals. I couldn't wait for them to be over so we could speak. As promised, as soon as rehearsals ended, Adebayo showed up, but he didn't show up alone. Zion was in tow.

I took my time packing my things to allow the rest of the band members to clear out. Something told me we were going to need privacy.

Finally, I made my way over to them.

"Hey. What's going on?" I asked.

Adebayo crossed his arms and looked over at his son.

Zion didn't make eye contact.

"Well. Don't you have something to say?" Adebayo asked.

Zion finally spoke. "Well, I … umm …"

But Adebayo wasn't playing with him, and his voice was stern. "Use your words, son."

"Miss … ahem… I mean, Amina," Zion said so low I could barely make out what he was saying. He shifted uncomfortably from one foot to the other. "There's something I need to share with you."

I glanced around at the few stragglers still in the room. I held my arm toward the lone office on the premises. "Let's go inside so you can speak freely."

We made our way inside the room, and I closed the door behind us. "Let's sit," I offered.

"I'm good, thanks," Adebayo answered.

Zion, however, accepted my offer. He leaned forward and

rested his elbows on his thighs as he finally spoke loud enough for me to understand. "I made a huge mistake. I'm sorry."

I wrinkled my brow. He still wasn't making sense, but I didn't let on to my frustration. "Okay. About what?" I urged.

"I may know what happened to that missing money in your account."

Adebayo furrowed his brow and crossed his arms. "You *may* know?"

"Okay, I *do* know what happened."

I took a deep breath to calm my nerves as I waited for him to continue.

He took a deep breath and his shoulders slumped. "It was me. I planted the device to spy on you. We initially planned to just get money out of the safe, but when we discovered your passwords for the bank and whatnot, we decided to get that instead."

My eyes grew wide. I even became speechless for a few moments, but it didn't take long for me to find my voice as I felt anger taking over. I stood up as my body became tense and I felt my nose flare. I began to talk with my hands as I grilled him.

"But why, Zion? Don't you know how much trouble your father could've gotten into because I blamed him? And who is *we*? Why would you do something like that to *me*? I don't understand."

He closed his eyes and shook his head. He shrugged. "I really don't know. I—"

Adebayo didn't wait for him to finish. He smacked him on the back of his head.

I gasped. Not only because I didn't believe in violence, but I'd never seen Adebayo act like this. "Oh, you know. You *need* to tell her the truth, Zi."

Zion grabbed the back of his head. "Dang, Dad. Okay!" He paused. "Well, there's this older woman."

"Okay."

"We've been kickin' it and whatnot. I met her several months ago. She's pregnant and said we needed the money for the baby. I was ashamed I got a woman pregnant *and* had just gotten laid off from my job. She came up with the plan to get your information so we could … you know …"

I raised my eyebrows. Oh, I knew. Never in a million years did I think something like this would happen to me. Especially with someone I genuinely loved and cared about. I never did anything more than welcome this young man into my life, and this is what I got? To say I was disgusted would be an understatement.

"Wow. I can't believe you would do this, Zion. Is it even *your* baby?"

"I think so …"

My emotions were bubbling to the surface. I shouted as I threw my hands up and glanced between Zion and Adebayo. "Zion! You *think*, or you *know*? Don't you think you should've known for sure before you started listening to this woman's claims?"

He nodded.

"Well, how far along is she?" I asked, as if it made a difference.

"She said she's almost four months."

I shook my head furiously. "Hmm. Have you even seen a pregnancy test or gone to a sonogram appointment?"

He shook his head. "No, not yet."

"You do realize that stealing is a crime, right?" I asked.

He lowered his eyes. "I didn't think it would go this far. She promised she would only do one transfer. And now I'm beginning to think it was less about the money and more about messing with you."

I sighed in frustration, but I wasn't surprised that his indiscretions were linked to a woman. "How did she even know the safe was there, Zi?"

He avoided eye contact as he spoke again. "That day I came over to your house to drop something off with Dad. I went to use the bathroom ... your door was open, so I peeked in. Your room was so nice, I wanted to see it more, and I went inside. I opened your huge closet and thought wow! This is dope! Then I discovered the safe. The light bulb was her idea. I switched it out that day I came to the BBQ at your house. Then I managed to grab the debit card and checkbook when I was helping Dad move. I also snapped pictures of your banking information in the safe. I almost changed my mind, but when you and my father broke up, I saw how hurt he was. It made me upset, so I decided to go through with it."

I didn't want to believe it, but I was hearing correctly. His words continued to shock me. Although I was upset with Zion, I was even more upset with this woman for taking advantage of him.

I glanced at Adebayo. He stood stoically with his arms crossed as he watched our interaction. He wore a pained expression, and I felt for him. I reckoned he probably didn't know what to say to all of this himself.

"But Zion, you hurt your father too. Don't you know how much trouble he could've gotten in?"

He nodded. "I do now."

"Well, where did you even meet this woman?" I huffed.

"I met her in front of your house. She was parked across the street. She saw me coming out of your house, said she was lost and needed directions ..."

I nodded but was unnerved that this woman knew where I lived. I paced as I tried to figure out what to do next.

Adebayo walked over to me and put his hands on my shoulders. He looked into my eyes. "I'm so sorry about all of this."

We both turned and looked at Zion.

I said, "Me too, but I know this wasn't easy for you. Thanks for letting me know."

"What do you want to do next?" Adebayo asked.

If it was anyone but Adebayo, I would've had him arrested immediately. But since Zion was Adebayo's only son who *might* have a baby on the way, I decided to give him a chance to redeem himself.

I went over to Zion. He kept his eyes diverted.

"Where's your phone?"

"Why?"

"I need you to call her."

He looked up at me in astonishment. "And say what?"

"Tell her you want to see her tonight."

"She's not going to like being ambushed. Plus, she's upset with me anyway. In fact, we've been getting into it because I refused to help her take any more money from you," he added as if he was doing me a favor.

I glanced at Adebayo; he looked at his son pitifully and shook his head. No doubt we were both thinking the same thing. Young and dumb. We picked up on the fact he was most likely being used by this woman but didn't want to burst his bubble.

Adebayo walked over to him and echoed my sentiments. "Do as she says. Call your little girlfriend right now!"

"Dad ... I don't think—"

Adebayo didn't wait for him to finish. "You should've been *thinking* about your dumb decisions before you made them. Call her ... *now!*"

Zion whipped his phone out at warp speed and dialed her number.

"Put it on speaker," Adebayo ordered.

Zion begrudgingly complied with his father's demands.

Three rings later we heard her voice. "Hello?" She sounded so sweet; I didn't want to believe this was the heffa that was making my life a living hell.

"Hey, Shareese. How are you?"

"What do you want, Zion?" she asked, clearly annoyed.

Zion glanced at his father.

Adebayo mouthed, "*Say something.*"

"Umm, do you mind meeting me by my father's house later this evening? I want to talk to you about something."

"You made it quite clear what you *weren't* going to do the last time we spoke. There's nothing more to say. Stop wasting my time."

"Please, Shareese. I want to make this right … for you and my baby."

"The only way we can make this right is if you do what we originally discussed and help me take the bitch for everything she has. This little chump change we took won't go far."

Adebayo and I glanced at each other again. Our fears were confirmed. She was *definitely* using him. My heart dropped to my knees. I still couldn't understand why this woman hated me so much.

I replayed the words "take the bitch for everything she has" in my mind. But why? It just didn't make sense.

Zion dropped his head. "Okay, Shareese. You win. We can hit a lick one more time, but then I'm done because we won't be able to take care of our child if *both* of us are locked up."

The line went silent momentarily, but it didn't take her

long to reveal her excitement. "Really? You'll do it? You don't know how much this means to me! I'll meet you around six at your father's house this evening. You won't regret it! I'm going to do something special for you tonight."

They hung up and I wanted to throw up.

# 23

## Anger, not Love

The longest hour of my life had finally passed. The moment was upon us as Adebayo and I sat in my car down the block. You never realize how unprepared you are for a situation until you are officially in that situation. The peaceful, calm Amina who always believed in giving many chances was put on ice. I had made up all kinds of scenarios in my head about how it would go when I saw this young woman. I planned to keep my cool as I normally did. She had two chances to tell the truth, but if she said anything I didn't like, by the third, I was about to show her why they called me 'Badass.'

But when she stepped out of her car, all thoughts of decorum went out the window.

The dress she wore was so tight, I couldn't imagine how she even got into it. But it wasn't the dress that made me zero in on her appearance. I recognized her face. It was the face of the woman who had tormented me at my gig, my mother's funeral, and lately, my dreams.

"That's *her*!" I exclaimed.

"That's *who*?" Adebayo asked.

"The woman. The woman who's been messing with me."

He wrinkled his brow and stared at me quizzically. "What are you talking about?"

"I'll tell you later, but that's *definitely* her."

"Umm, okay," he answered.

I thought about calling the police, but what could I say to them other than that she booed at me and showed up at my mother's funeral? I needed more proof.

We watched as she walked to the house and the door opened, signaling Zion had let her inside. Now, I was ready to pounce.

We waited a few moments before making any moves. After about five minutes, I was good to go.

"You ready?" I asked.

"I'm ready," he concurred.

We made our way to the door and the unsuspecting woman inside. I couldn't wait to confront her.

Adebayo opened the door, and I followed close behind.

She was shocked when she spotted us. She jumped up from straddling Zion and shoving her tongue down his throat. One of the loops of her dress straps was hanging from her shoulder, and her breast was almost completely exposed. She didn't attempt to hide it.

Adebayo played the surprised role. "What's going on here?" he asked.

She shouted at Zion, "I thought you said no one was coming home!"

I crossed my arms and shook my head when I saw her face clearly. It was most definitely *her*. Seeing her up close and personal made my stomach churn.

At first, she didn't seem to notice I was there, but when she spotted me, a devious expression ran across her face. "Oh, the non-singer is here too."

My blood boiled. I wasn't sure which Amina she would get if she kept disrespecting me. "Look, little girl, I'm not about to play with you tonight."

A smug expression ran across her face. "Isn't that what you do though? You play with people's lives?"

"What … what the hell are you talking about?" I asked.

Finally, she pulled the wayward strap of her dress up and tightened it. "You really have no clue, huh?" she asked snidely.

"If I knew, I wouldn't be asking, now, would I?" I threw back.

"Well, well, well. The ever-calm Amina ain't so calm when something is being done to her, huh? Maybe you need to light some candles?"

Her words gave me pause. This girl knew way more about me than I would've liked. I was becoming increasingly uncomfortable in her presence. I shifted my weight from one leg to another before I spoke again.

"All I know is that you have one minute to tell me why you've been stalking me, and what you've done with my money. I want it back. Now!"

It wasn't so much the money that had me reeling. I couldn't remember a time I felt more violated than in that moment.

Adebayo looked confused. "Stalking?" he said to no one in particular.

She put her hand to her chest as she feigned innocence. "Stalking. Me? Never that. And what money?"

I felt myself quickly unraveling. "Never mind," I said and began to walk away. I put my hand on my phone to call the authorities.

Adebayo grabbed my wrist gently and made eye contact with me. "Let's see if she'll tell us something first."

I glanced at him, then took a few deep breaths before speaking again. "Listen, I want to know what your problem is with me. You don't even know me."

She threw her head back and laughed, placing a hand on her hip. "Oh, I know enough."

"Well, I don't know anything."

She rolled her eyes and pursed her lips. "Oh, I wouldn't say that."

"What … are … you … talking … about?" I asked through gritted teeth. I didn't have any more nerves left for her to get on.

She scowled and pointed in my direction. "I'm talking about how *you* ruin lives! How you take what doesn't belong to you."

I threw my hands up and walked away. Frustration was clouding my judgment. In a minute, she wouldn't have to worry about me. If she wanted it that way, we could let the police open their line of questioning about how she robbed me.

Thankfully, Adebayo took over. "You might want to give us something to work with. She's about to turn you in."

"I don't owe you anything," she said as she grabbed her purse and attempted to go around him.

He stepped in front of her. "No, but you owe her," he said and gestured to me.

She glanced between me and Adebayo, then crossed her arms. "I think it's the other way around. *She* owes *me*."

I glanced at Adebayo. I could tell his patience was also wearing thin, and I was done with her games. I pulled my phone out and got ready to dial the three numbers that would change her fate.

"Look, I'm trying to help you. This is your last chance. Next, it will be the police," Adebayo said.

"Call them." She shrugged casually then pointed at Zion. "But, if I go down, so does he."

We hadn't thought that far ahead.

A look of horror ran across Adebayo's face. He looked over at me. His eyes pleaded with me to not make the call.

If it was anyone else, I probably wouldn't have listened, but the truth was, I felt that I owed him that. After all he'd put up with over the years from me and my dealings with Khalil, I owed him the courtesy of trying to keep his son from seeing the inside of a prison cell. Besides, he didn't have to tell me what happened in the first place.

I put my phone in my pocket and stood in front of the door. I crossed my arms. "Okay, we're listening. What do you *think* I owe you?"

Suddenly, she became demure. Almost childlike. "You can never give this back to me, but my mother's happiness would be a start."

# 24

# Damaged by Love

Again, we all were stumped by this young woman's words.

"Your mother's happiness? Who's your mother? What are you talking about?" I asked, throwing my hands up for the umpteenth time that night. If I had high blood pressure, I would've stroked out by now.

"I thought you would've been able to figure it out, but I guess I have to tell you *everything*," she said.

I crossed my arms and waited.

"My mother, Sydney Carter."

I paused and squinted in her direction. I couldn't believe I hadn't picked up on it earlier. She looked *just* like her mother. Now it made sense why I thought she reminded me of someone in the club that night.

"You're *Sydney's* daughter … ?"

She spun around and did a pose. "Yep, in the flesh."

"But, why?"

She sat on the couch, put her purse down, and crossed her legs. "Are you serious? Because *you* destroyed our whole family. That's why!"

"But … you weren't even born when I met your mother."

"No, but my mother tells me when Mr. Khalil left to be with you, it almost broke her. She was never the same."

"But she moved on and got married."

"Yeah, to my no-good father. When Mr. Khalil left, she left town and jumped into the arms of the first man who showed her affection. He left us high and dry though. She had to figure out how to make it with two children."

"What? Two children?"

"Yes, my older brother is even more messed up than I am about it."

My body stiffened as I glanced around the room. I was speechless. Me taking Khalil from Sydney all those years before had altered their universe. I never stopped to think how hurt she must've been when he left her for me. I never thought our love would've changed the course of other people's lives the way it did. In some way, maybe I did have a part in this mess. Maybe I deserved some of what Shareese was dishing out.

Thankfully, Adebayo jumped in. "Whatever happened between your mother and Khalil is in the past. That is their business. Not yours. Things happen in life." He looked over at me. "And sometimes, even though we're not happy with the situation, we learn how to adjust and move on."

I felt every word he was saying. I was sure he was referencing himself as well.

"That's all good and well, but now that Mr. Khalil has come back into my mother's life, they can finally have their well-deserved chance. But here Amina is again, inserting herself where she doesn't belong." She threw her hands up. "Why can't you just let them be?"

"I'm not—"

But she was far from done. "That's why I made it my mission to mess with her life, just like she did ours. You took from my mother, so I had to take from you."

Adebayo continued to try and reconcile the situation. "Your mother wouldn't want this for you. She'd want you to be happy. To find your own life's path, not live in hers."

Finally, a lone voice came from the other side of the room. "Are you even pregnant?" Zion asked.

We all turned in the direction of the voice. For a moment, I'd almost forgotten he was there. I hated that she had dragged him into her mess. *Our* mess.

She was callous. "You think I'd *ever* let myself get pregnant from a loser like *you*? You can't even keep a job!"

Adebayo was visibly upset, but it was Zion's aggression that alarmed us.

He lunged for her.

"No, Zion!" Adebayo yelled as he managed to jump

between him and Shareese moments before Zion could get to her.

"You're a dumb ho!" Zion yelled.

"Call Khalil and tell him to bring her mother!" Adebayo yelled, dragging Zion away kicking and screaming.

I dialed Khalil's number. Unfortunately, we were going to need more than Adebayo and me to put this fire out.

Thirty minutes later, Khalil and Sydney knocked on Adebayo's door. I hadn't given much of an explanation on the phone, except that we had an emergency and needed them to get there as soon as possible. A room full of broken-hearted exes. All because of me. We had all been hurt because of love, and I was the common denominator. I should've known that nothing good would come from all of us being in the same space.

When I opened the door, my heart dropped to see her standing beside him. Supposedly they were dating, but seeing him with someone other than me was painful. I guessed that's how he felt all those years I was with Adebayo. I imagined myself standing in her position but quickly reminded myself it was my fault that I wasn't there in the first place.

From Khalil's stance, he felt the tension as well. I hoped everyone would behave. Today was more than enough drama for me.

"Hello, Khalil ... Sydney," I said as I opened the door and moved aside for them to come in.

"Hello, Amina," they both said in unison.

It didn't take long for Sydney to spot her daughter sitting on the couch. "Shareese! What's going on here? Are you okay?" she asked and hurried over to her.

Khalil stayed close behind her.

"Thank God you're here, Mom! I was *so* afraid, and they wouldn't let me leave!" she lied and sprang off the couch into her mom's arms. Then she went over to Khalil and hugged him.

I rolled my eyes at her performance.

"He tried to hurt me. He was going to put his hands on me!" she cried. I did a double take and watched as the crocodile tears fell from her eyes. Oh, she was *good*!

"Who did?" Sydney asked.

Adebayo resurfaced, thankfully without Zion.

Shareese spotted Adebayo and pointed in his direction. "His son, Zion."

"Wait, what? You know it didn't happen like that!" I fussed.

Sydney wasn't having it. The quiet woman who had let me slide throughout the years pretending like she didn't exist, and flirting with Khalil in her face, quickly transformed into a mama bear. She did exactly what I had done to her on many occasions and turned the tables on me. She pretended like *I* didn't exist.

She turned her attention to Adebayo. "Is this true? Did your son attempt to assault my daughter?"

He took a deep breath and focused his attention on her.

"Like Amina *just* said, that's not the way it happened. If you'd just take a seat and let us explain what's going on, we—"

"Oh, so now you're calling my daughter a liar! Did your son try and harm my daughter, or not?" she pressed.

Adebayo looked like a fish out of water. "Your daughter has been—"

"Oh no. So, you're blaming her for *his* indiscretions? You're over here raising woman beaters?" she asked.

This situation was quickly going left. I took a deep breath. "Sydney, if you'd just calm down, we can tell you what—"

She looked at me like I was gum on the bottom of her shoe. "Don't you dare tell me how to act. You have *no* grounds to speak to me!"

I stared at Khalil, but he remained silent. Normally, he would've taken up for me, or at least said something. Anything would've been better than what he was giving now. But he said absolutely nothing. He just stood there with his new family. I was too through with him.

"You'll be hearing from my lawyer," Sydney huffed. She grabbed her daughter's hand and headed toward the door. Khalil wasn't far behind.

"Khalil?" I called after him.

He briefly found his balls, stopped, and spoke lowly. "Give it a few days and things should blow over. Give me a few days to talk to her."

Then he put his balls back in his pocket and followed the women out the door.

# Relentless Love

The next few days for me were a blur. I needed some time away to reflect and find myself again, so I packed a bag and spent most of my time hanging with Talia and her family. I witnessed firsthand the love between her, her husband, and their daughter. They reminded me of Khalil and me in the beginning ... long before we forgot why we had taken a chance on love in the first place. Long before our marriage had become complicated, and we'd let the pain of old wounds take over. I missed him. I missed us.

Shareese had gotten one thing right: I did ruin lives. I had hurt Sydney, Khalil, and Adebayo. Love wasn't supposed to hurt, but I always found a way to do just that. I made people hurt. I didn't want to die alone like she had told me in my nightmares.

While I was at my daughter's home, I picked Dr. Leon from the list of therapists Joy had sent over, scheduled his first available appointment, and had my first session with him. It was finally time to face my emotional trauma, and I knew I couldn't do it alone. I needed professional help. Shortly after my session with Dr. Leon, I headed home.

When I pulled up to my condo, I gasped. The words *Old Homewrecking Ho* were spray painted in black across the door, and I spotted broken glass sprinkled across the doorframe.

I took a deep breath and blinked back tears as my heart rate sped up. I slowly exited my car because I wasn't sure if I should approach the door alone. There was no telling what else Shareese would do to me if she continued to go to these lengths to ruin my life. I shook my head and took another deep breath before slowly moving toward the door. *I got myself into this mess, so I don't need anyone to get me out of it.*

I heard the crunch of broken glass with each step I took, and I cringed. My head and my heart hurt. I knew it was foolish to step on broken glass because of the threat of injury, but I didn't care. Maybe I deserved the pain since I had inflicted enough pain on others. It would serve me right if one of the shards of glass managed to bore its way through my shoe and rip my foot apart, just like I had ripped out so many hearts before.

I took another deep breath, slowly stuck my key in the door, turned it, and went inside.

I did a quick survey of my place. Thankfully, nothing seemed to be moved. Unfortunately, my insides felt just as messed up as the outside of my home.

I sat on my floor, crossed my legs, and closed my eyes. To say I was mentally exhausted would be an understatement.

A sound startled me, alerting me to the fact that I was not alone. My eyes sprung open when I realized I hadn't locked my front door.

A figure emerged. I squeezed my eyes shut as I knew I was about to pay with my life.

I didn't bother to scream as I prepared for what was to come.

After a few excruciating moments, I opened my eyes when I realized I was still breathing.

The bowlegs I always admired were standing in front of me. The light from the window revealed his handsome face. He broke into an awkward smile.

Khalil stretched his hand out. I reached up and put my hand in his. He grabbed my hand and pulled me up off the floor.

We both stared at each other with nothing but silence filling the space between us.

Finally, he spoke. "Damn, someone *really* doesn't like you, huh? What the hell is up with your front door and all that glass outside?"

We both shared a nervous laugh. "It's called Hurricane Shareese."

Frown lines creased his forehead. "No … really? You think so?"

"I *know* so. Who else would it be?"

"But why? I don't understand why she would do something like this."

I rolled my eyes and began to fluff my couch pillows. "Well, as the paint on the door suggests, I'm a Homewrecking Ho, right? That's what I was trying to tell you the other night, though no one was listening."

"About that—"

I held my hand up. I was too exhausted for his explanation in that moment. "Anyway, what brings you here? I never thought I'd see you here again. I figured you'd be with your *new* family."

He smirked before coming over to me and grabbing my hand. He sat down, taking me with him. "I felt bad about the way everything went down the other night, and how I haven't really been there for you like I should've been. When you didn't answer your phone today, I decided to drive by to check on you. I got worried when I saw the graffiti on your door, and when I tried your door and it was unlocked, I was afraid someone could've broken in."

Oh, so he *did* notice he was being a pussy the other night.

"Plus, a little birdie told me that you and what's-his-name were over."

Someone talked too much, but in this case, I appreciated it. "And who would that be?"

"Anisa."

I smirked. "Yeah, you left me hanging. You didn't speak up. Hell, you didn't say anything. Damn, Khalil. What's happened to you?"

He didn't make eye contact when he spoke. "I was trying to move on with my life."

"Seems like you were doing a pretty good job," I added sarcastically.

I wasn't going to pretend I was okay with how we left things after the intervention for Anisa, or him leaving me hanging the other night. Even still, I understood his wanting to move on.

"Well, I apologize for that. I was wrong. I was unprepared to deal with Sydney's blow-up. I've never seen her like that. But when it comes to our children …"

"All bets are off." I finished for him.

He nodded.

"Well, since I didn't get a call from the police, I guess you were able to call off your dog?"

"What do you mean?" he asked.

"Sydney. She was planning to press charges against Zion."

"By the time we got to the car, Shareese had all but gone back to being carefree and pulled out her phone to make a video for Instagram. For someone who had almost been assaulted, she didn't seem the least bit traumatized about the situation. She didn't even mention it again when her mother inquired about the details. I told Sydney I needed to speak to you about what happened."

"Mm-hmm."

He put his hand on mine and squeezed it gently. "I'm here now, and you have my full attention."

I gave him the rundown of what this young woman had done to me over the past few weeks. From her booing me at the club, to showing up at my mother's funeral, and admitting she had pulled Zion into her scheme of setting me up and stealing my money.

He shook his head. "And now your home. All because I left her mother for you all those years ago. Wow!"

I nodded. "She's hurt. I get it." I used my pointer finger to draw a circle in the air. "But all of this is too much."

"And the radio show? Do you think it was her the hosts were referencing? The person who said you ruined their family? Do you think she was speaking about us?"

To my chagrin, he had heard it. My eyes widened at his confession, and I nodded. "Quite likely."

"Damn. I'm sorry all of this happened to you."

"Me too."

"This is a tough one. I can understand why you haven't reported it yet. How do you plan to move forward?" he asked.

"I don't know yet, but this is the last straw. I'm starting to think of ways to get Anisa to beat the little bitch down. Just like she did Terrence." I was only half joking.

His eyes widened. In all the years he'd known me, he probably never heard me talk that way. *He* was always the one who wanted to put hands on someone. All I knew was if I didn't do something, her shenanigans would continue.

"I know you're not going to like this, but if I can get her to leave you alone, get the money back to you, and pay for the damages to the house, do you think you can walk away from this?"

I never thought I'd see the day when Khalil would side with Adebayo. They were both begging me to not report Shareese. They had different reasons, but it all boiled down to keeping her out of jail. Adebayo was her rock and Khalil her hard place. Between the two of them, I just couldn't win.

I smirked at the irony. "Can you also get her to give my good reputation back?"

We both laughed uncomfortably. It was my last attempt at taking a dig, but Khalil wouldn't hear of it. I guess a part of him felt he owed them too.

"No matter how you feel about her, she's still Sydney's daughter. She's dead wrong, but I still care about her and her mom. Let's just try first … Please. You're a mother. Imagine if it was one of our girls."

I rolled my eyes. He was getting soft in his old days. The old Khalil didn't play. He believed in justice, even if he had to take it into his own hands. Fortunately for him, I was still in love with him.

"For the record, our girls would *never* do what she did, but okay. I'll let you handle it your way. I'm warning you though. This is her *last* chance."

He nodded.

"And I know you may not believe in it, but repeat after me. She *needs* professional help."

He nodded again. "Okay. I agree. She needs professional help. Thank you. Thank you for trusting in me again."

"There's just one more thing that's been bothering me," I said.

"What's that?"

"Since when did you start allowing women to answer your phone?"

"What are you talking about?"

"Come on now, Khalil. You and Sydney ... I knew you two were dating and all, but when I called the other day, she picked up. Even *I* never did that."

"Wait ... Sydney answered *my* phone?"

"Yes. She said, and I quote, 'He's busy. He says he'll try to get back to you in the next few days.'"

"None of that makes any sense. I don't remember seeing a missed call or a text from you, and she never told me you called."

"Well, I can promise I *did* call, and I *did* text. When I didn't hear back from you, I figured you were done with me. I figured that was my cue to leave you alone ... for good this time."

He shook his head. "Amina, you should've known better. It doesn't matter what we go through, you know that I would never *not* care what's going on with you. For God's sake, you're the mother of my children!"

He wrinkled his brow. I could tell the wheels in his head were spinning off their hinges. "I just can't imagine Sydney doing that though."

In a few short moments, the answer hit us like a ton of bricks. We both looked at each other and spoke in unison. "Shareese."

We both shared another awkward laugh.

"Oh, she's something else," I said.

"That she is, but it doesn't matter at this point."

Now I was confused. "What do you mean?"

"It means I've tried on many occasions to walk away from us, but I can't. Honestly, I tried to make it work again with Sydney, but I can't. Because she's not you."

My eyes widened at his admission and my neck grew hot.

He continued, "You and I, we used to share everything, and I ... I miss that."

As much as I wanted him in my life, I was afraid to try again. "But ... Khalil, suppose I can't give you what you need? Suppose I can't—"

He cut me off by grabbing my hands and staring into my eyes. He kissed both of my hands. "Look, I finally understand what went wrong all those years ago in our marriage. I now understand when you say I wasn't attentive, and I was selfish." He paused then shook his head. "*Especially* in the bedroom. I was too wrapped up in trying to provide that I forgot about taking care of your needs. I also should've been more understanding when you told me how you felt after I got caught kissing Sydney that day. Especially when I knew what happened to you with Malcolm. I reduced your feelings to it only being a kiss and me having a moment of weakness. That wasn't fair.

It's not an excuse, but you and I were arguing all the time, and she was familiar. I should've heard you when you said you needed more from me. I broke your trust and took your love for granted. Now I understand why you sought comfort elsewhere and why you became jealous of Sydney. Not that it wasn't messed up, but I get it now."

I looked away from his intense stare. I was ashamed of the way I had handled things back then as well. Every time I remembered the hurt in his eyes when he found out I had cheated with Adebayo, my heart broke.

He lifted my chin to make me focus back on him. "*Both* of us played a part in the demise of our marriage, and it wasn't fair for me to only blame you. You being in my life is what I *need*. All I *need* is to hear you're willing to try. I can take it from there. I'm willing to do whatever it takes to make this thing work."

I paused. "The experts say statistics show relationships don't usually work out the second time around."

He laughed and moved closer to me. "When have you ever believed in that crap? Amina Thompkins never plays by the rules, right? Let's make our own."

"Hmm. Make our own rules, huh? That sounds like something my therapist would say." I paused and chose my next words carefully. "I started seeing one recently, and I really like him."

He nodded. "Oh, really? Sounds like a smart man. Well, maybe *we* can see him together."

My eyes widened and my heartbeat sped up in hopeful anticipation of what we could be again. "But you always said you don't believe in therapy."

"Like I said, whatever it takes."

I nodded.

"Does that mean yes?" he asked.

I didn't want to be foolish and think my desires for non-monogamy would disappear altogether, and I also didn't want him to resent me if I wasn't able to live up to his expectations. But this man loved me. I could tell by the way he looked into my soul. And now he was willing to do what it took to have me. No matter what happened in our lives, we always found a way back to each other. Him finally admitting he had played a part in the demise of our marriage was what I needed to hear, but his voluntarily agreeing to us seeing the therapist together was the icing on the cake. His words gave me hope. Hope that *both* of us would do what we had to for this to work this time. Hope that I could trust in our love and let it take us where we needed to go. I loved this man beyond reason, and I never wanted to be without him again. I was willing to try if it meant having one of my best friends and lovers back in my life.

My eyes filled with tears. "Yes. We can take it slow. Let's—"

He silenced me when he pressed his hard body against me and put his lips on mine.

My body went limp in his arms. I returned his kiss fervently.

We never made it to the bedroom. He made love to me right in the middle of the living room floor.

After several rug burns, and a few hours later, we lay in each other's arms. It felt as if his heartbeat was in sync with mine. No one could make me feel the way he did. Through all the mess, I had gained one victory, and he was lying beside me. I took comfort in knowing that before I snuggled closer to him and finally allowed sleep to take over.

# 26

# Don't Panic, Love

Unfortunately, our moment of bliss didn't last long. Our rest was disturbed later that evening with a phone call. Anisa's best friend, Monique, was on the other end.

I barely answered before she went in.

"Excuse me, Mrs. Thompkins. Sorry to be calling you at this time, but it's Anisa. She's in the hospital."

I sprang up in my bed. "Anisa? What happened? Which hospital?"

"Miami Regional. I'm not sure what's wrong. She said she was having trouble breathing, then she passed out, so I brought her to the closest location I could find."

"Okay, we'll be there shortly," I said before I threw my covers off and shook Khalil. "We have to go! Anisa's in the hospital," I exclaimed.

Like me, he was up and ready in moments. Together we

headed out. It felt good being able to roll over and not have to stop anywhere to pick him up for a family emergency this time.

We got in the car, and I called Talia and Nia to let them know where we were headed.

When we got there, the doctor informed us of what was going on. Anisa had had a severe panic attack. I didn't need anyone to tell me what could've brought that attack on, either. Dealing with months of stress from her job and Terrence had sent her spiraling out of control. Thankfully, it wasn't life threatening, and she was going to make it.

That didn't stop the tears from falling when I saw my baby lying in a hospital bed though. I kicked myself for being so wrapped up in my mess. I wasn't there like I should have been for her, even though I was aware of what she was going through with Terrence.

When she opened her eyes and looked at me, I smiled and rushed over to her. "Hey, queen," I said and hugged her as if it was the last time.

She turned to her father next. "Daddy, what happened?"

He bent and kissed her forehead. "You're going to be okay, princess. It was just a severe panic attack."

The doctor came into the room. "How's the patient?"

"I'm okay, I think," she said as she tried to sit up.

"Hold on." I hit the button to raise her bed.

When the doctor left, Monique poked her head in the door. "May I come in?" she asked.

"Of course, you can," I answered.

I was happy Anisa had friends like Monique in her life. Monique was to her what Joy was to me. She was her ride-or-die.

When her sisters arrived, my heart smiled. They hadn't spoken much since the so-called intervention we attempted to have at Anisa's house.

The one good thing about this moment was that it brought them out. I swear death and hospital visits could change the coldest of hearts. It was a reminder that any of us could be taken at any moment.

I pretended not to listen as she, Nia, and Talia made up. I watched as Talia and Anisa hugged.

"I'm so sorry," Anisa said with tears in her eyes.

"No, sis, I'm sorry. I should've never told you what you should be doing with your life. You can make your own decisions, not to mention I don't know what I would've done if something would've happened to you and we never had the chance to speak again." Talia held on to her sister for dear life.

Even Nia joined in. "I'm glad you're okay too. What the hell happened anyway?" she asked.

I almost envied this moment with the sisters, as I didn't think I would ever be able to get close to my sister again.

I wanted to ask Monique what they were doing before Anisa's panic attack but decided to leave that for another time.

Although the doctor assured us Anisa would be fine, he wanted to keep Anisa overnight for observation. I agreed that was the best thing for her, and Khalil and I decided to leave her there for the night.

The next morning, I went to the hospital bright and early to take Anisa home. As we waited for the nurses to come back in the room and give us the clearance for us to leave, I got a call from Kareem.

"Hey, Auntie Amina. Have you had a chance to check your messages today?"

"Hey, nephew. Sorry, I probably don't have the best signal where I am. I'm at the hospital getting ready to take your cousin home. What happened?" I asked.

"Talia told me. Thank God Anisa's okay. Give her a big kiss for me. But as soon as you get a chance, please check your messages. It's kind of important."

"Okay ... well, let me check it since I have you on the phone."

"Okay, cool."

I found his message and clicked the link for the news report he had sent me. The commentator said, "Major Instagram Influencer Shareese Carter was arrested last night for bank fraud. She's been accused of stealing thousands of dollars from several public figures, including the famed star Amina 'Badass.'"

Anisa and I stared wide-eyed at each other. She said, "What the ... ?"

My mouth dropped. "Kareem, what the hell?" I asked.

"I told you Instagram is good for something, Auntie. She

has almost a million followers and made a song flaunting how she can take money from anyone. The police began investigating after the song was released. Basically, she told on herself."

I was flabbergasted. As I'd said before, social media could be a blessing and a curse. I didn't understand this new generation.

What I did understand though, was I didn't have to do anything else to get justice. This young woman was too bold, and now the Universe was finally giving me a break. Adebayo's and Khalil's attempts to protect someone who thought she was invincible were futile.

Anisa shook her head. Her response was simple. "Dummy."

# Love From the Grave

dropped Anisa off at her home, then swung by mine. When I got there, there was a package addressed to me at the front door with no return address. I picked it up and flipped it over to see if there was something I was missing. When I saw nothing, I reluctantly dropped it inside my bag and went inside. I silently prayed that no one else hated me enough to want to kill me. I sat and slowly peeled open the envelope and pulled out its contents.

Surprisingly, I recognized the handwriting—I hadn't seen it in so long. I went to the kitchen, poured a glass of wine, and sat down because I knew I was going to need something to help me get through this. The letter read:

*April 18, 2021*

*My dearest Amina,*

*I hope you're not reading this letter anytime soon from the date I'm writing it, because if you are, I'm already deceased. I figured this time was coming sooner than later, so it had to be written. I've been feeling sick for some time now, but I didn't want to worry anyone. I mentioned not feeling well to your sister, and she wanted to take me to the doctor, but honestly, I didn't want to know what was wrong with me. I figure whenever the Lord is ready for me, he will call me home. I also don't want to die in some nasty hospital.*

*The letter you're reading now is most likely from my estate planner (btw, thanks for planting that seed so I could get my affairs in order). Without your encouragement, I probably wouldn't have thought to do this. His name is Ronald Jefferson, and his number is 786-549-0293, but I'm sure he'll be reaching out to you at some point soon enough. I don't have much, but whatever I have is for you, your sister, and my grandbabies.*

I took several sips of my wine after reading the first paragraph because I wasn't sure if I could continue. But I pressed on.

*I decided to write this because I've been a coward. I've been afraid to face you, my own daughter, because I've been awful to you. My problems have everything to do with me, and nothing to do with you. Please don't believe that mess I said about my issue being with you because you weren't singing for Jesus. I love the Lord, but I couldn't care less about where you sing. If you ask me, using your God-given talents is what God wants, and you don't have to do that in a church. Every time you open your mouth, and I hear you sing, I know that can be nothing but God. Your voice heals souls. Besides, your spirit is so beautiful, I'm sure God lives inside of you. I know some of those miserable church folk wouldn't agree, but it's not about them. Don't ever let anyone tell you otherwise.*

My eyes widened. I took a few deep breaths, then another sip.

*The truth is I look up to you, my beautiful daughter. I also wish I'd had your courage to stand up to my mother when I was growing up.*

My hands began to shake. I accidentally spilled some of my red wine onto the letter. "Shit!" I said as I jumped up to get a towel. Thankfully, the letter wasn't fully ruined. I put the wine down because I couldn't afford to *not* read her words.

I sat back down and continued.

*Yes, I said it. I know that may have caught you off guard, but I really mean it. I truly look up to you. You are the person I was afraid to be. You aren't afraid to live your life the way you want no matter what people think about you. I admire your fight, and your spunk. In fact, you remind me a lot of myself when I was younger. Unfortunately, I let my mother put my light out.*

*You probably feel like your sister is my favorite, but it isn't true. I love you both the same (actually, you are my favorite, but don't tell her I said that).*

I laughed through my tears and blew my nose. My mother was a trip. There was no doubt Jackie's letter probably also said *she* was her favorite.

*I know you don't think I'm serious about you being my favorite, but I mean it. You're probably laughing, huh? See, I know you better than you think.*

I laughed harder.

*Jackie was just easy. I didn't have to do much for her to follow what I wanted for her. I love my daughter dearly, but I swear she is the biggest kiss-ass.*

More laughter.

*I'm glad I can make you laugh. You deserve it.*

*But seriously though, there's no excuse for my behavior, but this is why I was so hard on you. I wanted to save you from the pain I felt when I attempted to be myself and folks turned their back on me. I was afraid to live my truth. If you don't know by now, you and Jackie have different fathers. I was in love with Jackie's dad but cheated with yours. When Mom found out, she forced me into a marriage I never wanted to be in. In fact, like you, I never wanted to be married. I wanted to be free as well, but that was unheard of in my day. Your father and I both had other partners during our marriage, so honestly, he wasn't to blame for our separation. We wouldn't have made it regardless because the love wasn't there.*

I stopped reading to wipe my eyes and blow my nose again. After a moment, I picked the letter back up.

*Oh, and I'm so damn proud of you and what you've done*

*with your life, especially your singing career. My daughter is a bomb-ass artist. Don't think I wasn't tuning in when you were interviewed either. I even snuck into a performance or two with the band. The way you work that stage. Girrrrl!!!! You're in a class of your own. You definitely inherited your mother's pipes too!*

I cried so hard, I could barely read the words on the paper.

*You're an AMAZING mother, and you deserve everything good. And, if you don't listen to anything else I say, listen to this:*

The next section of the letter was highlighted in bright yellow, as if I needed more than Mom's insistence that her words were important.

*You and Khalil are meant to be. Please try and work that out. You don't have to marry the man again, but you know you two shouldn't be apart. I see the way the two of you look at each other after all these years. If you two do decide to do it again, you can come to a middle ground. I'm sure he'll put in overtime this time to keep you satisfied as well (wink wink). A man who loves you enough will figure it out. Oh, and that Adebayo guy is nice, but he's just not right for you.*

I shook my head. This woman. Even in death, she found a way to be dramatic, but I loved it. I was definitely her child.

*Don't be mad at your sister. It was my fault that you two were divided. I made her feel like she had to choose. She really didn't mean any harm. Hopefully you're still speaking, but if not, please talk to her again. The two of you are all each other has and you need each other. Never forget that. Oh, and tell her crazy ass to let Kareem take that damn check. She knows her ass is broke, and money don't grow on trees. I don't know what I was thinking that day. Don't worry, your letter is also written specifically for you. Jackie got enough from me when I was alive (smile).*

*And last, but not least: If you can, please find a way to forgive me for everything. Know that I love you more than anything in this world.*

After reading her last words, I sat still and let the tears run down my face. Those words were all I ever needed to hear from her. Sometimes a mother's approval was all a girl needed. I felt a hundred pounds lighter. The letter also cemented that I was on the right path in my life's journey.

Finally, I folded the letter before placing it in my drawer.

"Thanks, Mom. I love you too."

# Back to Love

"Come on Iya, we have to get to the airport. We're going to be late!" Talia fussed as she stood by the door.

Anisa and Nia were outside. They had put the last of the luggage in the car and were waiting for me to lock up so we could make it for our flight to LA for the BET awards show the next day.

"Okay, I'll be right out. I have to pee, so I'll meet you in the car!"

I used the bathroom and grabbed my purse, but as I went to go out the door, Kareem walked in with his mother. I rolled my eyes. We needed to talk, but I didn't want to do it now.

"Hey, where did you two come from?" I asked.

"You've been avoiding me, so I wanted to catch you. Kareem said you all were leaving for a flight to California today."

I shook my head. I loved my nephew, but I wished he had

kept his mouth shut about my trip. "Jackie, we're running late. I have to—"

"I just need a minute."

Kareem leaned against the door and pulled out his phone. He pretended not to be listening as he scrolled through it. I would get him later, and I smirked at his measly attempt to ignore me and his mom.

I checked my watch. "Okay, I'll give you two."

She nodded. "The way I treated you after Mom died … and the way Mom and I handled the situation with our fathers was wrong to say the least."

I nodded. Mom was right about us needing each other. Now that things were finally falling back into place in my life, Jackie was the only missing piece to make everything feel complete.

"You deserved much better. You should've never found out about our dads that way."

I nodded again but said nothing. She was right. I loved her, but I just wasn't sure if I could trust her.

"Mom's letter. She asked me to forgive her, then myself."

My eyes filled with tears. I knew it wasn't her fault. She was caught up in our mother's mess too. All I wanted was us to be close again. She was my only sibling. She was all I had left from our mother. It was time to call a truce. Maybe we could take our time and start over.

"I miss you, and I'm sorry … for everything."

I pulled out a tissue and handed her one. I wiped my eyes.

"I miss you too," I said before we embraced. A horn honked, startling us and reminding me that we had to go. "Okay, as soon as I get back, I'll connect with you. But there's just one thing I want, and all is forgiven."

"Okay. What's that?" she asked.

I went to my desk table, wrote a check, and walked over to Kareem. I handed it to him. "I want Kareem to have this."

His eyes bulged when he saw the amount. He glanced between the two of us before he asked, "Are you sure, Auntie A? This is *a lot* of money."

Jackie glanced at it and shook her head. "Amina, we can't—"

"Mom insisted. Five from her, and five from me."

She broke into a smile, then nodded. "You're something else. You know that?"

"So I've been told."

Kareem bent and hugged me tightly. "Thanks so much, Auntie Amina. You're the best. I love you."

"You better! I love you too."

"Okay now. I see you, Mel! Who is this beautiful *young* woman on your arm?" the reporter exclaimed.

Mel squeezed my hand then kissed my cheek as we walked the red carpet for the BET awards pre-show. "Come on now.

You know I only hang with the best. This is none other than the amazing and illustrious Amina 'Badass!'"

I blushed and cheesed as well. I saw how he got his radio job. This man was *good* with the words. And that deep voice admittedly made my panties wet.

I looked good on his arm. Hell, *he* looked good on mine. I didn't take it for granted that I still looked this good at my age. It felt amazing to be able to hang with the young folks in and out of the gym, and it felt even better to know I still had it.

My three daughters weren't far behind.

"And who are these beautiful ladies with you today?" the reporter asked.

This was my first time attending an awards show, but since people were streaming my album like crazy, I figured the most I could do was show up and show out. That, and my daughters insisted I go. "This is a once-in-a-lifetime event, Mom! Next year, it might be you up there accepting an award. You need to get used to attending these events," they told me.

I'd missed getting picked by a mere few points for a new category for one of the most streamed album awards in which the fans could pick the album they liked most. I didn't mind though. I just felt honored to have been thought of. Anisa was right. This "Homewrecking Ho" was raking in the streaming sales.

I liked to think it was simply because my album was amazing, but I secretly acknowledged how the scandal had contributed to my album's success. I already had tour dates lined up for next year as well. Shareese's hateful tirade was more helpful than hurtful. But I pitied the young woman. I hoped she was getting the help she needed.

I pulled my daughters in close before pointing each of them out. "Well, these are my three beautiful daughters. This is Talia, this is Nia, and this is Anisa."

"Wow, you all look more like sisters than mother and daughters! You have a beautiful family!" the reporter exclaimed.

I blushed then winked at her. "Thanks. So I've been told."

We all shared a laugh.

She paused and tilted her head sideways. "Anisa ... aren't you a singer too? I heard something about you also being able to blow."

Anisa blushed. "Yes. I am. I just got back into it, but I'm loving every minute. Every now and then, I even sing with my mother's band."

"Nice! The apple doesn't fall far from the tree, I see." The reporter laughed.

"I guess you can say so." Anisa grinned.

We snapped a picture and then I spotted a familiar face. "Oh, I see a friend. Do you mind?"

"Of course not! I'll see you all inside," the reporter said before she made her way to another person on the carpet.

I turned to Mel and my daughters. "I'll be right back. Let me go and say hi."

When we made eye contact, Adebayo grinned ... hard. He

was looking very handsome. He had an unknown woman on one side and Zion on the other.

I went over to Adebayo and his crew.

I wasn't surprised to see him there as he had played a huge part in the making of my album. His expert drumming could be heard throughout most of my songs, and he deserved to be there as much as I did.

His date was gorgeous. I was elated for him.

Conversations with him had been scarce since our last encounter, so this would be a perfect time to catch up. At least, as much as you could on the red carpet with other folks around.

We embraced. Then he introduced me. "This is Amina. You know, the amazing songstress I played drums for."

I was glad he didn't bother to speak further about our past affiliation.

His date smiled and put her hand out. "Wow, I'm honored to meet you. He plays your album all the time."

"Well, thank you. It's good to meet you as well, … ?"

"Lauren," he finished for her.

Zion looked hesitant, so I reached over and pulled him into a tight embrace. He seemed relieved as he hugged me back.

I had long since moved past what he'd done. I wasn't even upset anymore. I was just glad to see him and his father looking healthy and happy. I was especially happy to see Adebayo had moved on.

We spoke some more, before he grabbed Lauren's hand and said, "Oh, did you see Lauren's ring?" My eyes widened when I noticed the ice sitting on top of her finger. "I proposed last night."

"Oh, wow! This is gorgeous. Congratulations!" I grabbed her finger and inspected the ring. I guess I wasn't the only woman who made him want to get remarried after all.

"Thank you so much!" She beamed.

We got ready to go inside. Adebayo and I embraced again, but before he let me go, he whispered, "Thanks for dropping the charges against Zion. Thankfully, they just gave him a slap on the wrist."

I winked. "I trust he learned his lesson."

He nodded. "Oh, and who's the new guy? He looks even younger than me. Where's Khalil? Don't tell me you've already kicked him to the curb."

I winked at him again. "You know I like to spice it up from time to time. And you know I don't talk about my love life," I teased.

He chuckled and shook his head. "Same Amina. I know. I'll leave it alone."

# EPILOGUE
## Love Reimagined

Khalil and I sat in Dr. Leon Blackwell's office for our first therapy session together.

Dr. Blackwell grinned. "It's very nice to meet you, Khalil. I've heard a lot about you."

Khalil nodded. "It's nice to meet you as well. And, same here."

"So, Amina, it's been several months since you first came to see me. But, by the looks of things, it seems as if the two of you are back together again?"

Khalil and I exchanged glances. My legs were crossed, and I leaned on him as he rested his hand atop my thigh.

I grabbed Khalil's hand before speaking. "We're dating. We're doing the work. We love each other immensely, and he's being extremely patient with me. While we haven't put a title on it, it feels like that's the direction we're headed in."

Dr. Blackwell crossed his legs and scratched his chin. "Well, good for you both! I'm happy to hear that."

I laced my fingers with Khalil's. "Yes, it's important that we heal from past hurt. But we're healing together, not apart. The past few months have taught me more about myself than I've known all my life. My mother also told me we can find a middle ground if we really want it to work."

"Awesome, so you finally spoke to her?" Dr. Blackwell asked.

"Umm, something like that. She died ... several weeks ago."

His eyes widened. "Oh no! I'm so sorry to hear that! How are you dealing with your loss?"

"I'm good, doctor. In fact, things are finally falling back into place in my life. I might even be falling back in love with love."

"Well, good for you! I'm so happy to hear that, Amina."

"Doc, you'd be surprised to know that I *may* be okay with her having a friend every now and then," Khalil added.

"Oh, is that so?" Dr. Blackwell asked with raised eyebrows.

"Yes. *But* we'd have limitations. The middle ground is she can go out with them, but she can't engage in sexual activity. I'm not there, doc. At least not right now. However, I'm no fool. If or when I can't fulfill her sexually, she can do as she pleases. For now, though, if it helps keep our sex life spicy for her to go out and flirt with some of these young studs every now and then, I'm down. She comes home ready, and I'm willing. We've also been incorporating more fun things into our sex life ... toys, porn ... whatever it takes. I figure, better late than never, right?"

Dr. Blackwell nodded. I'm sure he'd seen a lot in his days

of practicing, but I didn't know if he'd ever seen folks quite like us.

"*And* I'm free to date as well if I choose," Khalil threw in.

"He is. Anyone *except* his ex, Sydney."

We all shared a laugh.

"Honestly though," I continued, "it's true when they say people fear what they don't understand. Most folks won't understand our relationship, but it's not for everyone to comprehend. People need to do what works for them. Men who cheat like to say they never told a woman they wanted to enjoy other women because we just couldn't handle it. I say you just haven't met the right woman for the job. We women get bored with monogamy at times as well, but society has taught us we should think otherwise."

I squeezed Khalil's hand. "But it's all about communication. Honestly, between my children and grandchildren, my work, and him, I feel so fulfilled I rarely think about that anymore though. At this stage of my life, I don't feel like I'm missing anything. Especially since I've realized that in my case, my issues with love and relationships were because I wasn't getting the love I needed from my mother."

I glanced at Khalil. "Especially when we started having issues in our marriage. The fact that he's willing to love me beyond what he's used to makes me love him even more. This version of Khalil who's making it his duty to meet my needs is all I ever wanted. Now, I also want to do the same for him."

Dr. Blackwell nodded. "That's how it's supposed to be.

Both parties striving to meet each other's needs. Serving each other."

We both nodded.

"I'm keeping you on speed dial if anything changes though, and I'll be sure to let Khalil know when he's slippin'. And I want him to do the same for me. We could've saved ourselves a lot of heartbreak if we would've just slowed down and talked about how we both felt during our marriage. So, this time around, we promised to sit down together and reevaluate our relationship goals every few months."

"Okay now! I really like that. I have one more question though."

"Sure," we answered in unison.

"Khalil, how did you feel about her looking all cozy on the red carpet with that young man. Mel, is it?"

Khalil glanced at me. "Oh. We discussed it beforehand. I don't want to attend that stuff anyway, so he was the perfect decoy. Let everyone think those two have something going on. Those folks don't matter. I trust her enough, plus it's all about what happens when she comes home to me."

I nodded, but I wasn't sure if I agreed. I didn't want to hide how I felt about him anymore.

We got up to leave, but before we went out the door, Khalil stopped me. "One sec, sweetie. I'll be right back."

He made his way over to Dr. Blackwell. I watched as the two of them shared a few moments of friendly banter. I pressed my ear into the room to see if I could hear what they were talking about. They spoke low, but I could make out what they were saying.

Dr. Blackwell handed him a card.

Khalil cheesed like a kid in a candy store as he read it. "So, you say this doctor can prescribe some safe male enhancement drugs? Not that I need it and all, but I'm sure it can't hurt." He stepped back and beat his chest. "Thankfully, I'm still holding my own, but I may need a little backup with this one. Her sex drive stays on ten!"

Both men laughed and shook hands.

I covered my mouth to keep from bursting out into laughter.

Khalil made his way out of the office and grabbed my hand. "Shall we?"

"Sure, my king."

When we made it to the house, we got ready for bed. I was ready for some private time, but he stopped me short before I got too excited about the bedroom games.

"Amina, I have to tell you something. It's important that you know."

Immediately, my stomach churned with anxiousness. I nodded, leaned over, and kissed him deeply. "Can it wait? Let's just love on each other tonight," I said and batted my eyelashes at him.

He smiled. "Yes, ma'am. I love you."

"I love you more."

The next morning, we arrived at the radio station hand in

hand. I wasn't interested in doing the fake shit several celebrities would do by having their significant other walk behind them and showing little to no affection when they thought folks weren't watching to keep their love lives private. I understood the implications of people knowing the status of my love life, but I didn't care.

I had a surprise for Khalil. Something I'd wanted to do for some time now.

When we got to the room to do my interview, I spotted good ole Jameson first.

"Hey, Ms. Lady! So glad to see you back again. You ready for today?" he said as if he hadn't dragged me on his show just a few weeks before.

"Hey, Jameson. Of course. I'mma make it do what it do!" I laughed.

"Well, let's do it!" he exclaimed.

He spotted Khalil and did what most people did, but he was extra with his reaction. He licked his lips and put his manicured hand to his chest. "Well, hello, Mister …"

"Khalil," Khalil said and extended his hand for a handshake.

I chuckled. Jameson was smitten. I wasn't surprised though. I knew my old man was looking good.

Jameson batted his eyes and tooted his lips out. "Okay, well hello, *Khalil*."

Mel cleared his throat. He didn't seem pleased to see Khalil there. "Okay … cool, yeah. Umm, Khalil, would you mind sitting in the waiting room while we conduct our interview?"

"Oh no, he's with me. He can stay," I interjected.

"Oh … well, usually agents—"

"He's *not* my agent."

Mel's eyes widened. "Oh. Okay. My apologies."

"No offense taken," I said.

We exchanged pleasantries, then my interview began. Finally, Angel got the nerve up to ask about my *friend* who was with me that day.

I turned to him and blushed. "Oh, this is Khalil."

"Mm-hmm. We know how private you are about your love life, so should I dare ask?"

"It's okay. You can ask. In fact, let me do this." I stood up and threw my arms around Khalil's neck. "Come here, baby."

You could hear a pin drop as I kissed him deeply.

"Oh, my (beep) God. That's what the (beep) I'm talking about!" Jameson exclaimed.

"Aww, that's so sweet!" Angel said.

"That's just nasty" was Mel's response.

But I wasn't done. "Khalil, father of my children, and love of my life. We've been through so much. We've seen plenty of good and bad times. We've raised three beautiful daughters, have several wonderful grandchildren, and experienced enough highs and lows to last a lifetime. You've been my rock through it all, and I never want to be without you again. I respect you. I thank my creator for you, and I love you in more ways than I can count."

"Aww," Jameson and Angel crooned in unison.

Mel rolled his eyes at our exchange but stayed silent.

"Khalil Amir Thompkins, will you promise to continue being my partner in love?"

The three cohosts gasped. They thought more was coming, but I was done. I had shared just enough. It was no marriage proposal, but Khalil knew me well enough to know exactly what me showing my undying love for him in public meant. I was letting him know that I was finally letting my guard down and giving this relationship all that I could.

It was no one else's business the way we chose to do it.

He blushed then began to sweat. I'd put him on the spot, taking him out of his comfort zone. He wiped his forehead and stood up. He kept it simple. "Of course I will. And I love you too."

I was finally ready to take another ride on the roller coaster of love with him.

Our relationship wasn't traditional, but we found a way to have it work for us. We understood each other better than anyone else, and that made him my real soulmate. We were the true definition of what love should be: give and take and compromise. Loving Khalil was one addiction I never wanted to cure. When it came to him, I would always be a Love Enthusiast.

Thanks for tuning into the Amina Thompkins Love Show. I hope you've enjoyed your visit. Make sure you come back again soon for my next show. My daughter Anisa and I will be serving up the tea in the next edition. But, for now, go love on your special someone, and if you've enjoyed the show, please don't forget to leave a review and, or rating wherever books are sold and pass the word along!

Sincerely,
Amina 'Badass'

Two years later …

Anisa

# 1

I closed my eyes and tried to relax as the plane lifted off. I didn't particularly enjoy flying these days.

Zahair reached over, grabbed my hand, and squeezed it lightly. "Breathe baby, just breathe. It'll be ok."

I smiled. My heart swelled as I looked over at him. It felt good to be in this space.

I squeezed his hand back and laughed. "I know. I know … thanks my love, but I'm not giving birth. At least not yet."

I rubbed my belly as the plane began to level off.

The past two years with Zahair had been a whirlwind. Late night phone calls turned into weekend flights between Miami and DC. Both of us had racked up enough flight miles to fly all over the world for free. I never imagined that this would be my reality. I found myself spending more and more time in DC now that Iya had joined Devyn and I in sharing the responsibility of Iya's gems. I knew my girls would be in more than good hands with her. You couldn't tell her they weren't her own. She would tell everyone she met she had twenty-one children. Eighteen of them being the bonus children we gained from our organization.

I was barely showing, but the baby I always wanted would be born in seven months. We hadn't even shared the details with our families yet as we were waiting for me to make it out of the first trimester. We both admitted we'd made mistakes before when we attempted to be together. And Zahair even admitted he became too possessive, pushy even, after we had hooked up in DC. He realized he should've been more patient and promised to never leave or block me again.

I knew he just wanted the best for me, so we decided to see where our relationship could go. What I hadn't counted on, was being pregnant and unmarried. Baby aside, this was not something I would've asked for, because I'd seen many women including my sister, Nia struggle with it.

I didn't have the time to worry about that right now though. The main reason for me jumping on a plane was lying in a hospital bed.

My father, the first man who loved me, had had a major heart attack. I couldn't believe my daddy, stronger than any lion, had such a close brush with death. He now lay comatose in a hospital bed. Surely, if my mother hadn't been with him at the time, he'd be dead right now.

I shuddered to think about that because my daddy meant everything to me. He still wasn't in the best shape, but he was alive. That's all I could've asked for in a time like this. In my heart of hearts, I knew if anyone could make it through this, he could.

I took a few deep breaths.

"You, ok?" Zahair asked.

I smiled at him.

"Yes, my love. I'm fine."

He smiled back, then leaned his head in the seat and closed his eyes.

I did the same.

I was happy my family was there with my dad. I tried not to feel guilty about being away from my family all the time, but he was in more than capable hands with my mother and sisters there.

I was also happy that we were all getting along. My sister Nia and I had become even closer after I left, especially after my hospital scare. The part I was most excited about though, was that my parents were now back together. They had finally realized they couldn't live without each other. I couldn't imagine how broken my Iya must've felt after my father had that heart attack though, especially after finding their way back to each other a few years ago. I also didn't believe God would be cruel enough to take my father from her after all they had been through to get back there. Despite his condition, I believed she could love him back to life.

# REFLECTIONS OF IMPERFECTION

We are Amazing.

An outstanding reflection of imperfect beings.

Our love bonds us together as nothing else can.

With each breath we take, inspiration will lead us into another plane.

To bask in the depths of each other because this love we've found, is insane.

We study to show ourselves improved, but until the right time, we are not moved.

Because of our bond, transformation is destined to come. To all who see us and what we've become.

A true reflection of what can be. When two lovers experience transparency. I can see you, and you can see me.

When anger is present, we choose to fight fair. We will never let it take us into despair because our objectives are so clear.

When we come together, our bodies intertwine, as he

swims in my river. He becomes the force, and I, the giver. Our exquisite gifts to each other.

Though very different, our hearts are the same. I lean on his strength and he on mine. The empowerment we give each other is truly divine. We are one flesh.

We do more than hope because we surely know, if you don't take action, you cannot truly grow.

Where we are now is because elevation has taken place. Although it hasn't been instant, because we're in no race. We've taken time to know each other as only two souls meant for each other can.

Every day, we decide to wake up and choose each other again. Even when it's not easy, I know I can depend on him, giving me his all, and I doing the same for him. We will always be.

Thank you to everyone who continues to support me on my writing journey. Your unwavering support reminds me that dreams do come true.

**Visit Keisha 'WriteNow' Allen online:**

Instagram *@keisha_writenow_allen*

Facebook *@Keisha WriteNow Allen*

Visit my website: www.keishawritenowallen.com

Here you can:

- Find out about contests and prizes
- Find out more about my writing journey
- Learn about upcoming books and merchandise
- And much more